A strange voice came over the line. It sounded almost like a computerized voice, flat and distorted. But there was something human and threatening in the tone, something a computer could never be.

"Aloia. I know you took bribes from a booster. I have proof. And I'm willing to take it to the Ethics Board," the voice said.

Anthony's mother gasped.

"There is only one way to stop me," the voice went on. "You have to drop the ball on Saturday."

"What? What is that supposed to mean?" Mr. Aloia sounded frightened.

"It means he wants me to throw the game," Anthony said. "And I have to do it."

THE HARDY BOYS

UNDERCOVER BROTHERS®

Available from Simon & Schuster

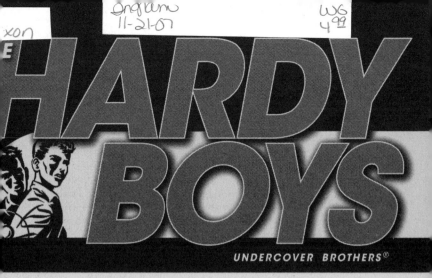

HARDY BOYS

UNDERCOVER BROTHERS®

#19 Foul Play

FRANKLIN W. DIXON

Aladdin Paperbacks
New York   London   Toronto   Sydney

❧ ALADDIN PAPERBACKS
An imprint of Simon & Schuster Children's Publishing Division
1230 Avenue of the Americas, New York, NY 10020
Copyright © 2007 by Simon & Schuster, Inc.
All rights reserved, including the right of reproduction in whole or
in part in any form.
THE HARDY BOYS MYSTERY STORIES and HARDY BOYS
UNDERCOVER BROTHERS are registered trademarks of
Simon & Schuster, Inc.
ALADDIN PAPERBACKS and related logo are registered trademarks of
Simon & Schuster, Inc.
Designed by Lisa Vega
The text of this book was set in Aldine 401 BT.
Manufactured in the United States of America
First Aladdin Paperbacks edition November 2007
10 9 8 7 6 5 4 3 2 1
Library of Congress Control Number 2007921737
ISBN-13: 978-1-4169-4977-0
ISBN-10: 1-4169-4977-1

TABLE OF CONTENTS

1.

Cat Attack

The tiger was asleep.

That was the first thing I noticed when I opened my eyes.

A sleeping tiger is better than an awake tiger, I thought. But there's no such thing as a nonthreatening Bengal tiger. And this one was about five feet away from me.

I could just see my brother, Joe, over the tiger's giant white head. And I could see metal bars all around us.

We were trapped in the tiger cage.

I ignored the pounding in my head and tried to recall how I got here.

Fearless must've gotten the jump on us, I realized. As in Fearless Fontana, Master Trainer. An

1

over-the-top Las Vegas showman. ATAC—that's American Teens Against Crime, the organization Joe and I work for—had sent us in to investigate Fearless and his business partner, Roland Pritchard. They suspected the two of running an underground animal fighting ring using their Vegas tiger act as a front. And they were right, as usual. Joe and I had discovered that Fearless and Pritchard made most of their money by staging animal fights between members of endangered species.

We infiltrated the "Fearless Fontana" act with me as an usher and Joe as a stagehand. It didn't take long to figure out that Fearless was slipping hidden messages into his snappy onstage banter. Half the time, it sounded like the dude was speaking in code. Because he was! Pritchard would sell the code key to his wealthy clients. Then they would go to the Fearless Fontana show, listen for the code words, and figure out where and when the next fight would be held. It was like a game to these sick people.

Joe and I had cracked the code for the next fight. It was between a Florida panther and a Canada lynx. And it was happening tonight. Maybe even right now.

I checked for my cell phone to look at the time, but my cell was gone.

Fontana must've jumped us, taken our phones, and stuck us in here so he could get himself and the animals to the fight on time.

A sound from behind startled me. I turned, slowly, to see a second Bengal tiger sleeping nearby. And snoring, with his gigantic mouth hanging open so that I could see each razor-sharp tooth.

Terrific, I thought sarcastically. *That one's even bigger than the first one.*

"Psst!" Joe waved, beckoning me over to the cage door. I sat up and backed away from the magnificent creature in front of me as quietly and carefully as I could. Then I inched slowly between the two tigers. As an usher in the show, I had learned to respect these animals.

The Bengal tigers were beautiful, with white fur marked by dark brown stripes. They were probably nine feet long and more than four hundred pounds each. Based on the size of these two, I figured they were both males. All in all, not the type of cat I wanted to mess with. Predators like this spend most of their days sleeping, but they can wake up at the sound of a pin dropping. If we could get the door open, we'd be okay. But if the cats woke up hungry . . .

It would be ugly.

The cage was large enough for the two big cats

to pace and play. I estimated it at twenty feet by twenty feet, with the top—also made of metal bars—about eight feet off the ground. It was in an empty room in the middle of a warehouse that had been turned into an exotic animal stable. Even if the tigers were awake, Joe and I could yell for help for hours and still not be heard. As it was, though, it was more important to be quiet.

When I finally reached Joe, I found him fiddling with the door.

"I need some metal," he whispered.

"Huh?"

"To pick the lock," he said, gesturing to the padlock he held in his hand. It was old, not meant to keep human beings in. Still, it wasn't going to just fall open on its own.

"My pocketknife doesn't have a thin enough blade," he told me. "We need something long and thin, like a needle."

"Fontana didn't take your knife?" I asked, shocked.

"He didn't find it." Joe shrugged. "I keep it in my shoe. Sometimes."

"Weirdo," I muttered.

Joe and I both looked around the cage, trying to find anything that might work. After a few minutes of searching, Joe gestured to me from the far corner. I started toward him to see what he had. But just as I stepped over the tail of the larger tiger, Joe took a sharp breath.

I glanced up to see his pocketknife falling through the air. He must've dropped it when he was trying to pry a sliver of wood off of a beam just outside the cage.

Clank!

The sound of metal on metal echoed through the huge warehouse. I whipped my head around to look at the big cat three inches away. His ears rotated slightly toward the sound and his tail began to trace a lazy arc along the floor. The other cat stirred too, but neither opened their eyes. I exhaled slowly . . . and noticed something.

The thick white leather collars the tigers wore for the show were still around their necks. I'd never seen them this close up before. It looked as if they were reinforced with thin strips of metal, probably to make sure that the cats couldn't rip them off.

If I can get to those metal strips, Joe might be able to make something with them, I thought.

I took a deep breath and held it, so I wouldn't accidentally breathe on the tiger's whiskers as I stepped gently toward his head. As I leaned down, I had to marvel at his size. His paws were larger than my feet, and his head was the same size as my chest. I studied the collar, which was held together by a heavy-duty clasp system. It looked kind of like the clasps on rock-climbing straps.

I knew how to work those clasps because Joe and I were expert climbers. Still, it wasn't gonna be easy. And I was already running out of air. Concentrating, I lifted the metal clip and slowly slid the leather out, expanding the collar. I checked on the tiger—so far, so good. I pulled the tongue out of the metal housing until it was fully open. That's when I realized what the really big problem was.

The open collar lay flat on the cage floor. But the tiger's massive head was still lying on top of it.

Just go for it, I told myself.

I pulled fast, trying to slide the collar out like a magician pulling a tablecloth out from under a full place setting.

But I'm no magician.

The tiger's eyes snapped open. He immediately lifted his huge head, his penetrating blue eyes boring into me.

Not good.

I tossed the collar to Joe, who was back at the cage door. He grabbed it out of the air and immediately began sawing the metal strips out with his pocketknife.

The movement of the bigger tiger must have triggered something in the smaller one, because he suddenly woke up as well.

They both stayed where they were. Staring at me.

"Hurry, Joe," I said cautiously and calmly. From watching the act, I knew better than to agitate these tigers. They were used to people, having been raised in captivity the way most white Bengal tigers are.

They don't seem very hungry, I thought, relieved. *Fearless must have been in too much of a rush to bother worrying about finding a cage with ravenous tigers to lock us in.*

Joe freed the first metal strip. He stuck it between his teeth and started on the second.

The smaller tiger lifted himself slowly up. He looked at Joe and lazily raised one paw to his mouth to lick. His tail swished back and forth. Putting the paw down, he took a step in Joe's direction.

It wasn't threatening exactly, but it wasn't friendly, either.

Then the bigger tiger sat up. He focused his blue eyes on my brother. His long tongue came out and licked his chops.

Joe ignored the tigers and kept working.

I knew it was up to me to keep them away from him.

I didn't have a whip or a chair, but I needed something to get the cats' attention. I pulled my belt out of my jeans and folded it in two with one end in each hand. I jerked my hands apart, snapping the belt to make a whip sound.

The tigers jerked their heads toward me. The big one stood up, staring at me. The other one turned away from Joe and took a step in my direction.

"Nice kitty," I said.

Slowly I backed up against the wall opposite Joe, putting as much space between the cats and me as possible. I snapped my belt again. Both tigers blinked. The big one growled. But they were used to whips. The whiplike sound kept them at bay for the moment.

The smaller tiger moved over to stand next to the big one. Now they were both directly between Joe and me.

Between me and the door.

"Got it!" cried Joe, holding up the second piece of metal. "This shouldn't take long." He stuck the metal into the padlock just as the big tiger took a swipe at me.

I snapped the belt again.

The tiger opened his gigantic mouth and roared, the sound making the metal bars vibrate against my back. But he took a step backward. The roar was still only for show.

The other tiger pinned his ears back, gazing at me intently.

My belt trick wasn't going to work for much longer.

The big tiger dropped into a crouch and took a step toward me. The other one walked to the side, circling around. My stomach lurched. These cats were hunting.

Hunting *me*.

"Let's go!" Joe threw open the door.

The big tiger pounced.

I had no time to think. I jumped up as the tiger went forward. Somehow I managed to get over his head. I swung my belt into the air, aiming for the bars at the top of the cage. One end went over a bar, and I grabbed at it desperately.

Just when I was about to land in the tiger's mouth, my fingers touched leather. I had one end of the belt in each hand, with a loop over the bar. I hung on tight, using my arms to pull myself up higher.

They can jump, a voice in my head whispered.

"Here, kitty, kitty!" Joe yelled from outside the cage. The smaller tiger turned toward him and stared, confused.

I swung myself toward the cage door and stuck one foot down, pushing off of the bigger tiger's back to get myself moving.

He snarled and raked his claws through the air about half an inch from my leg.

On instinct, I pulled my leg up and over him. The momentum carried me forward, sliding along the metal bar on my belt.

When I was two feet from the door, I used all my strength to hurl my body forward. I let go of the belt and flew through the air.

Out the door.

And onto the floor.

Joe slammed it behind me.

We both stared at the roaring, furious beasts in the cage. The bigger one had his entire leg between the bars, still trying to get me.

"Come on," Joe said. "We have to find a phone and call ATAC. They'll send the police to the endangered animals fight."

"Yeah." I frowned back at the two big cats. They had managed to get my belt down from the top and were tearing it to pieces.

"What?" asked my brother. "We solved the case. The police are gonna get the bad guys. Mission accomplished."

"I know," I said. "It's just . . . I really liked that belt."

2.

Big-League Mission

"Hurry up, Joe," my brother called through the bathroom door.

I ignored him and just kept swishing the Listerine around in my mouth. Frank is always in a hurry. I like to mess with him by taking my time getting ready.

"Fine, I'll just open this box by myself," Frank said. I heard his footsteps receding down the hallway.

A box? I thought. *As in a package from ATAC?* That could only mean one thing—a new mission. I spit out the mouthwash, jerked open the door, and tore down the hall to Frank's room. My brother sat at his desk, opening up a box . . . of doughnuts.

"It's just doughnuts?" I groaned.

11

Frank grinned. "I can eat them all if you don't want any."

"I didn't say that," I replied quickly. I managed to snag a Boston cream before he pulled the box away. The first bite tasted terrible because of the mouthwash. But the next bite was heaven. "Where'd you get the doughnuts?" I asked with my mouth full.

"From Vijay," Frank said nonchalantly.

I almost spit out my cream filling. "What? When?" Vijay Patel was an ATAC agent. He often brought us our mission assignments.

"He delivered them while you were in the shower." Frank finished off a cinnamon-coated cruller. "You should've seen him. He was dressed like an old-fashioned baker, with a big white hat and everything. He told Aunt Trudy that the Donut Hole was doing a promotion where they were giving away free doughnuts to everyone under the age of twenty."

"And she bought it?" I asked, surprised. Our aunt is suspicious of everything. And she's especially suspicious of things that are free.

"Not really," Frank said, laughing. "She tried to send him away. She said we don't need any more sugar in our diets. I thought Vijay's head was going to explode!"

I chuckled and reached for a jelly doughnut. "What did you do?"

"Oh, I just grabbed the box from him and took off running," said Frank. "I sprinted up the stairs before she could catch me."

"Wow," I said approvingly. "That sounds like something I would do."

"Yeah." Frank stuffed a sprinkle-coated chocolate doughnut into his mouth. "I bet she's complaining to Mom right now about us gorging ourselves on sugar."

"Like we'd do that." I threw two doughnut holes into the air and caught them both in my mouth.

Frank gestured to the box. "That's it for the doughnuts," he announced. "Want to check out what's underneath?"

"You know it." I closed the bedroom door while my brother peeled up the fake bottom of the doughnut box. Underneath were two little silver gadgets and a disc with the silhouette of a football player on the cover. Frank grabbed the disc and popped it into his computer while I studied one of the gadgets. "It looks like an iPod or something," I said.

"Shh, it's starting." Frank turned up the volume on the fast hip-hop music. On the monitor, a football flew straight at us, getting bigger and bigger until it filled the whole screen.

"Baseball is called 'America's Pastime,' but football is where the big money is," a voice said over the music. *"The big gambling money."*

The football disappeared and was replaced with an image of a giant board, the kind you see in Las Vegas casinos. *"Vegas oddsmakers keep track of statistics for all the major college football franchises,"* the voice went on. *"Betting on college games isn't legal in all states, but you can bet it happens anyway."*

"Hah! The ATAC announcer dude made a joke," Frank said.

"You're a dork," I informed him.

Aerial footage of a stadium filled the screen. The place was packed. *"The average attendance at a top-ranked college game is more than ninety thousand,"* the voice went on. *"The money from ticket sales and concessions from a single game is more than most students pay for tuition for all four years. The money from television and Internet broadcasting rights is greater still."*

The scene switched to a field-level view of a bunch of huge guys charging one another.

"For a college with a highly rated team, the income is substantial," the announcer said. *"Many people— from alumni, to members of the college board, to students themselves—stand to profit from a successful team. But when that kind of money is at stake, people's ethics often get shaky."*

The scene went to slow motion as one gigantic dude took out another one by grabbing the face mask on his helmet and yanking his head to the ground.

"*You've probably heard of Pinnacle College in Colorado,*" the announcer said.

"Go, Mountain Lions!" I cheered. Frank rolled his eyes.

"*The Pinnacle team has dominated the season in Mountain Division football this year,*" said the announcer. "*They are undefeated, and their streak is expected to continue in the divisional championship game.*"

"The championship game is a week from today." Frank sounded worried. "They're playing Miller State."

"You don't think . . . I mean, *that* can't be our mission, can it?" I asked excitedly.

"*Anyone who follows college football knows that the Pinnacle Mountain Lions are considered unbeatable,*" the announcer continued. "*So why have there been rumors trickling into Vegas lately that suggest the Mountain Lions may actually lose to their old rivals, the Miller State Warriors?*"

"Wait, the oddsmakers say Miller State will win?" I said, confused.

"*So far these are only rumors. The safe money is still on Pinnacle to win,*" the announcer explained. "*Nevertheless, we here at ATAC are concerned. There have been* no published reports of injuries to key players or dissension within the Pinnacle team. Basically, no reason for anyone at all to think the Mountain Lions won't win."

"Then where are the rumors coming from?" Frank asked.

"We believe it's possible that there is some inside knowledge of a plan to sabotage the championship game," the announcer stated. *"It's the only reason for such supposedly unfounded rumors."*

Frank gave a low whistle. "ATAC thinks the Mountain Lions are going to throw the game on purpose."

"If a player—or many players—intentionally loses the championship game, they would be defrauding the university, all its financial boosters, and anyone who placed legal bets on the game. Not to mention anyone who purchased tickets to the game or pay-per-view TV rights."

As the announcer spoke, a picture of the Pinnacle stadium popped up, followed by a group picture of some guys in suits, a Vegas casino, and finally a bunch of people watching a game on TV. A big red *X* went through all of them as he finished his sentence.

"Your assignment is to go undercover as Pinnacle College students for the next week," the announcer summed up. *"The head coach, Tip Orman, is aware of this mission and will help you blend in with the team. It's*

up to you boys to discover what's really going on behind the scenes at Pinnacle. If somebody is planning to throw the game, you have to find out who. And stop them."

"We'll have to tell Mom and Aunt Trudy we're going on a ski trip or something," I said.

Frank nodded. "Dad will help us with that." Our father, Fenton Hardy, is a retired cop. He is also one of the founders of ATAC. Which comes in pretty handy when ATAC sends us on a mission and we need someone to cover our tracks with Mom!

"In this box you'll find all the information we've gathered on the Mountain Lions, including complete dossiers on every team member. We've also provided you both with the latest technology from the lab here at ATAC. They may look like personal music players, but these are also highly sensitive recording devices that can pick up sound from fifty feet away. They function remotely, through walls, and in tandem. And of course, they play music."

I grabbed the little silver gadget and began examining it.

"You leave tomorrow morning for Pinnacle College. Good luck, boys. As always, this mission disc will be reformatted in five seconds. Five . . . four . . . three . . . two . . ." The images vanished from the screen, and the loud hip-hop blasted from the speakers again.

• • • •

"You the Hardys?" A gruff, broad-shouldered man asked us the second we stepped off the prop plane at the small Colorado airport on Sunday morning. The winter weather was freezing.

"Yeah," I replied. "I'm Joe and this is Frank."

"Tip Orman," the man said. "Follow me."

He led the way across the tarmac and into the tiny airport. There was a dingy coffee shop tucked away between the ticket counters and the bathrooms. Coach Orman sat himself down at a cramped table. Frank shot me a confused look, then sat down across from him. I squeezed in next to my brother.

"It's great to meet you, Coach," Frank said. "We've followed your career at Pinnacle, of course—"

"Save it," Coach Orman growled. "I'm the best there is and we all know it. We're not here to talk about me."

Frank shut his mouth, his cheeks flushed. But I laughed. This guy was no-nonsense. I liked him. "Why don't we talk on the way to the college?" I asked.

Coach Orman raised his eyebrows.

"Because the coach doesn't want anyone to see him with us," Frank put in. "It could blow our cover."

The coach nodded. "I can see you're the brains," he told Frank. He turned to me. "That means you must be the muscle."

I had no idea what to say. I was just as smart as Frank! But I also liked the thought of being the muscle. . . .

"You'll be a player," Coach Orman went on. "Nobody expects them to be smart."

"Hey," I protested. Then his words sunk in. "A player? On the Mountain Lions? Cool!" I pumped my fist in the air.

"My backup kicker is down with a bad knee," the coach said. "We'll say I brought you in to take his place. You're backup, so there's no chance you'll ever have to play. But you can come to practices and get to know the team."

"That's perfect," I told him. "It will give me an inside look at how the guys relate to each other. If any of them are planning to throw the game, I'll find out."

"What about me?" asked Frank. "What should my cover be?"

"I don't have any other open slots on the team," Coach Orman said. "I'm thinking we'll make you a manager."

"Okay. What does a manager do?" Frank asked.

"You'll help run the day-to-day. Keep track of

equipment and schedules, make sure everyone's pads are in good shape, run messages to the special teams coaches, keep the locker room clean, that kind of thing," Coach Orman explained.

Frank was silent.

"So basically he's like a secretary or something?" I said. "Or a janitor?"

"He's someone who has access to the locker room, the field, and the players," Coach Orman growled. "That's the best I can do."

"That will be fine, Coach," Frank said quickly. "Do you mind if I ask you what you think? I mean, you're cooperating with ATAC. So you must think there's something negative going down with the team, right?"

"Wrong." The coach ran his hand through his graying hair. "Look, your organization contacted me and I'm willing to help out. I don't mind if they want to send a couple of kids to snoop around, and I'll make sure your covers are good. But I don't believe for a single second that any of my players are going to lose this championship for us."

"Then why are the Vegas oddsmakers hearing rumors against you?" I asked.

"I have no idea," the coach said. "I don't understand how any of that gambling garbage works. What I know is football. And I know that the Pinnacle

Mountain Lions have the strongest offense in the league. Defense? Well, that's another story. I'd say we're only third- or fourth-ranked when it comes to defense. But it doesn't matter. My quarterback is the best, my receivers are the best, my star running back is the best, and my team is the best. We're unbeatable. I don't care what the Vegas gossip says."

Coach Orman pushed back his chair and stood up. "I'll expect you both at practice first thing tomorrow morning," he added. "You can get a bus to the campus from here."

He turned and left without even saying goodbye.

"Wow," Frank said.

"I know. He's not the friendliest guy in the world."

"The reporters always say he's a man of few words, but that the players really respect him," Frank noted. "I guess it's true. You don't have to be nice to be a great football coach."

I grabbed my duffel and headed for the door. "Let's go. I want to get to Pinnacle and get settled in. I've got a big day of practice tomorrow. I'm gonna need my rest."

"Like a kicker has to do anything physical," Frank teased me. "You're nothing but a bench-warmer."

"Better a benchwarmer than a glorified errand boy," I retorted, grinning. I shoved open the door and looked around for the bus to Pinnacle College. This was gonna be the coolest mission of all time!

3.

The Suite Life

"Let's go over it one more time," I said as the elevator creaked up to the fourth floor of Brazelton Hall.

Joe rolled his eyes. "We're transfers from a college back east—"

"Which college?" I asked.

"Annoying Brother University," he replied.

"If we don't have our stories straight, we could blow our cover," I pointed out.

"Fine. We're transfers from Bayport State, and I came here because Coach Orman wanted me to be a backup kicker. I don't know why *you* had to come along."

"We'll just say I'm here for the academics," I offered. "They have a strong math department. We can say I'm majoring in math."

"Whatever." The elevator jerked to a stop and Joe pressed the Door Open button impatiently.

"Remember, you're a freshman," I told him. "I'm a sophomore."

"Got it," said Joe. The doors opened, revealing a long hallway with greenish walls and ugly gray carpeting. My brother grinned. "Dorm life, here we come!"

I followed Joe to suite 412, where ATAC had assigned us to stay. According to the team dossier, the other guys in the suite were on the football team too.

"Your new roommates have arrived," Joe announced, pushing open the door. We were in a room with an old couch, two folding lawn chairs, and a huge TV. Off to one side was an open door leading to a bedroom with bunk beds. Directly across from it were another bedroom and a bathroom.

Two dudes were playing a video game on the giant TV. They didn't even glance in our direction.

"I don't think they're too excited to see us," I said to Joe. I glanced into the room with the bunk beds. "Should we just dump our stuff in here?"

"I guess." Joe turned toward the bedroom door.

But before he could take a single step inside, the smaller of the two dudes leaped up off the couch.

"No!" he yelled. "Stop!"

Joe froze.

The guy came running from the common room. "You have to step in with your right foot first," he said quickly. "Both of you."

"O-kay." Eyes wide, Joe stuck his right foot through the bedroom door. He went in and tossed his duffel bag on the ground. I followed, right foot first.

"Are we allowed to just walk back out, or do we have to reverse the whole thing?" I asked.

The guy looked at me like I was nuts. "No," he said. "It only matters on the way in. Duh."

By this time, the other dude had joined him in the entryway. "Don't mind Ken," he told me. "He has a superstition for everything. He thinks if you don't put your right foot first it means you're getting off on the wrong foot. I think he read that on a fortune cookie once."

"I did not," Ken protested. "It's just that I stepped in with my right foot first when we moved in here at the beginning of the school year. And the team hasn't lost since."

"The team hasn't lost ever," the other guy said. "That's because we're good. Nobody cares which foot you're on unless you're kicking."

"Kicking?" said Joe. "I'm a kicker too!"

Ken looked him up and down. "Oh, yeah?"

"Coach Orman brought me in. I'm the new backup kicker for the Mountain Lions," Joe explained.

"Ken here is the starting kicker," the big dude replied. "And I'm Luis. I'm the backup quarterback."

"I'm Frank Hardy, and this is my brother, Joe," I said. "Guess I'm the only nonplayer here."

"That's okay, we'll still hang with you," Ken joked.

"Thanks. I'm gonna be a manager for the team," I told him. "Got to keep tabs on my little brother here."

Joe shoved me. I shoved him back.

"You guys hungry?" asked Luis. "I'm thinking pizza."

"We can't do pizza," Ken argued. "It's Sunday."

Luis groaned.

"Let me guess, no pizza on Sunday because it's unlucky?" I said.

"The last time I had pizza on Sunday, I totally

missed an easy field goal," Ken explained. "I kicked it and it got blocked."

"Yeah, but we still won," Luis said.

"And if it got blocked, it wasn't your fault," Joe pointed out.

"It wasn't my fault, but it was my bad luck," Ken insisted. "So now I can't eat pizza on Sundays until the championship game is over."

"Isn't there a dining hall?" I asked. "We can just eat there."

"No!" cried Ken. "We can *never* eat in the dining hall."

"Don't even ask," Luis said, shaking his head. "The dining hall is like the evil vortex of all bad luck as far as Ken is concerned."

"You're really serious about this stuff," I remarked to Ken as Luis went into the common room and started looking through Chinese food menus.

"I just don't want to mess up our winning streak," Ken said. "The team is really important to everyone at Pinnacle. Everybody's school spirit is all wrapped up in us winning the game next week. I can't take a chance that bad luck will get in the way."

"Then I guess I shouldn't throw your lucky

sweatband out the window, huh?" Luis asked from the common room.

I turned to see him dangling a dark blue band through the open window, a wicked grin on his face.

Ken went deathly pale. "N-no," he whispered.

Joe was laughing. But I thought Ken might have a heart attack.

"Tell you what," I said. "You let us order pizza and I bet Luis will spare your lucky sweatband."

Luis raised one eyebrow. "Interesting. Forcing him to choose between two superstitions. Which one will it be, Kenny?" He shook the sweatband, fake-threatening.

Ken suddenly sprinted across the room and launched himself at Luis, tackling him to the ground. Luis looked so surprised that Joe started laughing even harder.

"Didn't you say you were the kicker?" I teased. "You looked more like an offensive tackle."

"I do what I have to." Ken grabbed the sweatband and stood up, stuffing it into his jeans pocket. "Now let's order some Chinese."

"I call the top bunk," Joe said when we headed into our room after dinner.

"Fine with me. Then I can keep you up all night kicking your mattress," I replied. I unzipped my duffel bag and pulled out the folder with the dossier of the football team. "We've only got a week. We need a plan."

Joe frowned. "There's a lot of guys on the team. It's hard to see why any of them would want the Mountain Lions to lose."

"I know." I chewed on my lip, thinking. "Maybe we can't start with motive. There are too many people involved. Maybe we should just figure out how they could throw the game."

"A boxer can throw a boxing match just by letting himself get hit and pretending that he couldn't stop it," Joe said. "And in a baseball game, if you get enough guys to agree to play badly, you can lose the game."

"Right. The pitcher throws easy pitches on purpose. And the catcher drops balls. And the outfielders miss catches," I added. "So how do you do that on a football team?"

"Simple," said Joe. "It's the quarterback. He's the one who calls the plays. He's the one with the ball almost all the time. So when he's doing a pass play, he throws the ball too far. Or he purposely throws an interception. When it's a running play, he lets himself get sacked. Or he fumbles the handoff. It's all about him. If he does a bad job, the team loses."

"Not necessarily," I argued. "If the quarterback starts throwing wild or getting sacked a lot, Coach Orman will just put the backup quarterback in instead." I tossed him the dossier. "Check out Luis's stats. He's a great backup quarterback. At most schools, he'd be the starter."

"So?"

"So . . . it doesn't have to be the quarterback. The running backs and the receivers are the ones who actually score. No quarterback is worth much without a good receiver."

Joe studied the players' statistics. "Well, they've got a few good receivers, but only one real star," he said. "Anthony Aloia."

"What about the running backs?" I asked.

"Easy. Marco Muñoz. He ran for over a thousand yards this season alone." Joe frowned. "But I still say you can't throw a game without the quarterback."

"Fine. You check out the quarterback. I'll take Aloia and Muñoz."

"Great. It's a plan." Joe grabbed on to the frame of the bed and swung himself up into the top bunk. "Now I'd better get some sleep. I have a tough day of football practice tomorrow. And you have a tough day of . . . cleaning out lockers."

I kicked the mattress above me.

"Ow," Joe complained. I smiled.

4.

Practice

"Coming through!" a huge guy bellowed from the showers. I stepped back to let him pass, and he ran by, trying to strap on his shoulder pads as he went. As soon as he was out the back door, I glanced down at the floor.

His cleats had left muddy footprints all over the floor I had just mopped.

"Why?" I said out loud. "Why do you run through the showers fully dressed?"

"Because you're late for practice, the shower door is the fastest way to the field, and Coach makes you do three extra laps for every minute you're late," a voice answered me.

I glanced over my shoulder to see a tall guy in a button-down shirt and khakis hovering in the

32

doorway that connected the showers to the main locker room.

"Okay, then," I said. "Why is there a *door* in the showers?"

He laughed. "It's supposed to be locked, and marked for emergency exit only. You know, in case of fire. It's a long way back through the locker room and the entire gym complex, especially if the place is burning down around you."

"I guess," I grumbled. "I didn't hear an alarm."

"Nah. I disabled it." He stuck out his hand. "I'm John Roque."

"Frank Hardy." I shook his hand. "I'm the new manager."

"Cool. I'm the old manager," he said. "One of them, anyway. Now that you're here, there are three of us."

"Yeah, I met Manzi," I replied. "He said he had to go pick up the away-game uniforms from the laundry. I think he just didn't want to mop."

Roque chuckled. "You catch on quick. You're gonna be stuck with a lot of the grunt work, I think. Manzi usually does all the cleaning because I'm more involved with the high-tech stuff. Coach doesn't get computers, but he wants all the players' schedules on his computer, and he wants the entire playbook there too, with lots of encryption."

"So you're a computer geek?" I asked.

"Computers, scoreboards, changing lightbulbs . . . anything that seems like it involves technology of some kind, Coach makes me do it."

"Hence disabling the fire alarm," I guessed.

"Yeah. But don't tell Coach about that," Roque said quickly. "The players know about it, but he doesn't. He'd make *me* do laps if he found out."

"Got it," I said. I stuck my mop in the pail of brown water and started mopping up the footprints. "I have to say, this seems pretty pointless," I commented. "I'm gonna get it all clean and then they'll come back in after practice and mess it up again."

"Get used to it," Roque advised. "You, me, and Manzi will be here for at least an hour after the players go home to get their beauty sleep."

"But why not just clean it all after practice is over?" I asked.

Roque shrugged. "That's Coach Orman's way. Everything has to be clean, organized, and under control. Including players. He runs a tight ship. Most of these lunkheads wouldn't know how to run in a straight line without him."

My eyebrows shot up. "Lunkheads? Are you saying the amazing Pinnacle Mountain Lions are lunkheads?"

Roque groaned. "Oh, don't tell me you're one of those guys who idolizes the football players."

"Well . . . I did volunteer to be a manager," I pointed out.

"Yeah, but isn't your brother on the team now? I figured you were just involved because of him."

"Basically," I admitted. "How did you know?"

He held up his PDA, a truly kickin' Sidekick. "I do the player schedules, remember? If a new kicker suddenly shows up, I have to know about it."

"Right. Of course," I said. "Truth is, my dad wants me to keep an eye on Joe. Pinnacle's team is big news. I think Dad is worried that Joe will get sucked into being a campus celeb and forget that he still has to actually go to classes."

"Your father is right. You wouldn't believe how many of these idiots are close to flunking out," Roque told me. "Anyway, I better go transfer these schedules onto Coach's desktop."

He turned to go.

"Hey, Roque," I called after him.

"Yeah?"

"If you think the players are such idiots, why are you a manager?" I asked. "You got a little brother on the team too?"

"Worse," he told me. He pointed to a poster-size black-and-white photo on the wall. A smiling Pinnacle player holding up a giant trophy. "My father was on the team."

My mouth dropped open. "Roque. Your father is Fred Roque?"

"*Doctor* Fred Roque now," he answered. "He went into orthopedic surgery after that broken ankle ruined his NFL career."

"Fred Roque was the quarterback during Pinnacle's best two seasons ever," I said. "Even I know that."

"Yup, he was a superstar." Roque grinned up at the photo. "He always wanted me to be like him. Go to Pinnacle, star on the football team. But it's just not my thing. I figured the least I could do was be involved with the team somehow. It makes him happy, you know?"

I nodded.

"You've got about half an hour before the first bunch come back to hit the showers," Roque said. "I'll be in Coach's office if you need me."

As he left, I looked down at the half-mopped floor. I hoped Joe was having a better time than me.

JOE

"I don't get it," I complained. "Why do we have to do the team drills? We're kickers."

"It's just for warm-up," Ken said. He was in

front of me in the line of seven guys. "Coach likes to remind everyone that knowing how to handle the ball is always gonna be the most important skill."

"Talk on your own time," Coach Orman bellowed from the sidelines. "We've got a championship to win." Instantly Ken turned his back to me. I figured I'd better shut up too. Coach might be willing to help ATAC with our investigation, but he obviously wasn't going to let me interfere with practice.

I shoved my shoulder pads to the left, trying to make them comfortable. I wasn't used to the extra weight. And my cleats were new, so they kind of pinched my feet. And, worst of all, I was nervous. This was a hugely successful college football team . . . and I had to pretend that I was a good enough player to be here.

Somehow I hadn't realized that I would be running drills with a bunch of humongous, NFL-bound twenty-year-olds. Would I be able to pull it off?

The drill was pretty basic, just a handoff from the quarterback. Well, for our line it was handoff from the backup quarterback, Luis. When I got to the front of the line, I took a deep breath and went for it. All my years playing football in school came back to me. I managed to grab the ball without dropping it.

"You stink," one of the big guys in front of me muttered when I got back on the end of the line. His jersey said "Orena" on the back.

"Lay off," Ken said. "It's his first day. He's nervous."

"He still stinks," Orena insisted. Then Coach Orman came around again and everybody shut up. But I'd already decided two things: Luis was fast at the handoffs, and Ken was my hero for sticking up for me.

I made it through three more handoffs before Coach stopped that drill. The rest of the players split up into offense and defense and headed off with their assistant coaches. The offensive coordinator told Ken and me to head over to the sidelines and do some practice kicks to warm up our legs.

As we jogged toward the side, I spotted Luis at the water keg along with another guy. I recognized his face from the team dossier—it was the starting quarterback, Billy Flynn. Just the dude I was looking for.

"You go first," I told Ken. "I want to see how it's done."

"You're supposed to come hold the ball for me," he said.

"I will," I promised. "I just need to get a drink first."

Ken shrugged and began doing kicks off a tee. I went straight for the water. "Luis! My man," I greeted my suitemate.

"Hey, Joe." Luis nodded.

"Who's this loser?" Billy Flynn asked.

"Joe Hardy," said Luis. "Meet Flynner."

"Hi." I offered my hand. Flynner ignored it. "I'm the new backup kicker," I added.

"We won't need you," Flynner stated. "I'll take care of all the scoring next week." He grinned. "Don't I always?"

"You know it," Luis replied.

"It must suck for you," Flynner said to Luis. "If I wasn't so good, you might get to play sometimes instead of being just a benchwarmer."

Luis shook his head. "Nice," he muttered.

"No, I mean it. Aren't you jealous of me?" Flynner went on. "You probably dream about the day I graduate so you can finally play."

"As long as we win the championship, I'm happy," said Luis.

"Yeah, right." Flynner snorted. "Well, you better enjoy it, because once I'm gone you won't be winning any more championships."

It sounded like typical trash talk, but I could tell

that Flynner was serious. He obviously thought he was some kind of football god. Luckily, I knew just how to deal with that type of guy.

"You really are the best quarterback in the league," I said. "Maybe even in all of college football."

Flynner squinted at me. "Yeah."

"I'm serious. You're incredible," I gushed. "You're the whole reason I wanted to transfer to Pinnacle. You were my football hero all the way through high school."

Out of the corner of my eye, I noticed Luis staring at me like I'd gone crazy. I ignored him. I finally had Flynner's attention, and that was all that mattered. So what if the guy was a jerk? I had to find a way to question him. I had to make him trust me.

"Thanks." Flynner grinned. "What's your name again?"

"Joe Hardy."

"Hardy. You're all right," he said.

Luis rolled his eyes, tossed his paper cup in the trash, and jogged off. It looked like Flynner was going to follow him, so I talked fast. "I probably shouldn't say this, but I am so psyched that your backup kicker got hurt. As soon as I heard about it, I started calling Coach Orman. It was my dream to be able to play on the same team as you, even if it's only for one game."

"I doubt you'll do any playing," Flynner told me. But he sounded sympathetic, not mean.

"I know," I said. "But I'll be out there wearing the same uniform as you, and I'll get to watch from the field while you work your magic."

He chuckled.

"I have a bet with my brother that you're gonna be the number one overall draft pick for the NFL after this championship game," I went on.

"You'll win that bet, my friend," said Flynner. "No doubt about it."

"So you're that confident we'll win, huh?"

"It doesn't even matter if we win." Flynner leaned closer to me and lowered his voice. "I've got an inside track. I'll be top overall pick. It's in the bag."

"An inside track?" I repeated. "You really are my hero."

And now that I knew he was involved in something shady, he was also my top suspect!

"Hardy!" Coach Orman bellowed. "Did I tell you to take a break?"

"Um . . ." I glanced up at Flynner. He spit some Gatorade on the ground.

SUSPECT PROFILE

<u>Name</u>: Billy "Flynner" Flynn

<u>Hometown</u>: Muncie, Indiana

<u>Physical description</u>: 21 years old; 6'1", 202 lbs; dark hair, blue eyes.

<u>Occupation</u>: Quarterback for the Pinnacle Mountain Lions; college senior

<u>Background</u>: All-state high school football champion; best quarterback stats in Mountain League college football.

<u>Suspicious behavior</u>: Admitted to having an inside track in the NFL draft pick.

<u>Suspected of</u>: Planning to intentionally lose the championship game.

<u>Possible motive</u>: Willing to throw the game in return for a guaranteed top spot in the draft.

"Don't look at me," he said. "I'm the quarterback. I can do whatever I want."

Coach stalked over, his face red. "You're here to practice, Hardy," he snapped. "Get out there and give me five laps."

Obviously Coach was planning to treat me like

every other player on the team. He probably didn't want to blow my cover. I tossed my helmet onto the bench and jogged over to the track. Five laps was more than a mile, but that wasn't too bad. Even with pads on, it shouldn't take more than ten minutes.

I ran kind of fast, trying to get it over with. It wasn't long before I spotted another guy up ahead, doing laps. He wasn't going too quickly—I could tell I was gaining on him.

As I drew closer, I saw that it was Orena, the big guy who had heckled me during the drill. I caught up and fell into step with him.

"Hey," I said.

He nodded, but didn't say anything. He seemed pretty winded.

"Why'd you get laps?" I asked.

"I was late," he grunted. "Three laps for every minute."

Harsh, I thought. From the way Orena was panting, I figured he must be on at least his fifth or sixth lap. "How many are you at?"

"Two," he gasped.

Two? The dude looked exhausted. Shouldn't an athlete be in better shape? I wondered what his deal was.

And then he collapsed.

"Whoa!" I dropped to my knees beside him. His eyes were rolled back into his head. "Help!" I yelled as I felt his neck for a pulse. "I need a doctor over here!"

But it was too late. There was no pulse.

Orena was dead.

5.

Dinner with the Enemy

"Murder?" Frank asked in a low voice. When the ambulance arrived to take Orena to the hospital, everyone was still milling around on the field. But I had booked back to the locker room to find my brother. We needed a private talk.

"How could it be murder?" I said. "There was nobody else around. The guy just dropped dead."

"Maybe someone poisoned him," Frank said doubtfully. "Or it could've been steroids."

"Nope, not steroids," John Roque put in. I jumped in surprise. I hadn't heard the other manager come over to us. I wondered how much he had heard.

"Sorry, didn't mean to scare you," Roque told

45

me. "I heard you guys talking about Orena. It wasn't steroids."

"How do you know?" Frank asked.

"All the players are tested every week. You know that, Joe."

I hadn't been tested. I wasn't a real player. But I went along with it. "Yeah, that's true. If Orena was on 'roids, Coach would have known it."

Roque tapped the earpiece for his cell phone. "Coach called from the ambulance. They stopped doing CPR. The EMTs say Orena was probably dead before he even hit the ground."

I nodded. The way the poor guy had collapsed . . . well, I could believe he'd died quickly.

"Coach talked to the team doc. They think Orena had some problem in his heart, something he didn't even know about," Roque explained.

"And the exertion of practice made it worse," Frank finished for him. "That's awful."

Roque nodded solemnly. "Anyway, Coach wants us to spread the word. This championship game is going to be played for Orena. We're gonna win for him. Tell everyone."

Frank nodded. "I'll get on it." He shot me a look and headed off to talk to the players, who were starting to trickle back in from the field.

The mood in the locker room was subdued.

Everybody was upset about Orena. "Did you know him well?" I asked Ken as we stripped off our pads.

Ken shook his head. "I'm not sure anyone really did. He was a freshman, so he wasn't a starter or anything. He'd only been a Mountain Lion for a few months. Still, he seemed like a good guy."

"Yeah." I tried to shake off the image of Orena falling down right in front of me. I still couldn't help wondering if his death was somehow connected to the reason Frank and I were here, but maybe it really was just an eerie coincidence. Either way, Frank and I would follow up later, make sure there was nothing more sinister than an unknown heart condition.

"Try not to let it get to you, Joe. We all have to stay focused," Ken said. "You had a good practice."

I raised my eyebrows.

"For your first day," he added. "Don't worry. Next season you'll really get into the groove. This week is just kinda crazy, with the big game coming up."

I only wished I would be here next season! "I guess," I said, trying to sound more cheerful. My whole body ached from the exertion of practice.

I didn't know how I was going to make it though the week.

"You want to hit the sauna with me and Luis?" asked Ken.

"Uh, no thanks," I told him, stealing a glance at Flynner. The quarterback was over near the office, talking to Marco Muñoz. I wanted to stay nearby so I could catch him on his way out.

"All right. See you back at the dorm." Ken disappeared into the mondo sauna with a bunch of other guys. My sore muscles wanted to follow him, but I had a mission to accomplish.

I shuffled the things in my locker around, trying to look busy while Flynner spoke to Marco. Finally he said good-bye and headed for his locker.

"Hey, Flynner," I called casually. "You hitting the sauna?"

"No way," he said. "Only losers need to keep their precious muscles warm."

"Yeah, that's what I think," I agreed quickly. "So you want to go get a burger or something? It's been a bad day. I'd love to hear some football stories to cheer myself up." I hated kissing up to this dude, but it had to be done.

Flynner slammed his locker shut and grabbed his gym bag. "You buying?"

"Sure." ATAC was buying, but he didn't need to know that.

"Then let's go." Flynner drove to a diner just off campus, and I followed him on my motorcycle. The second he pushed open the door, Flynner started yelling.

"You got hungry players in the house! Bring us cheeseburgers, stat!" He ignored the WAIT TO BE SEATED sign and led the way to a booth in the back. I tried to pretend I didn't see the other customers staring as I sat down across from him. "Waitress! I need a Coke!" Flynner bellowed.

I glanced around. There wasn't even a waitress anywhere near us. This guy was seriously obnoxious.

"I think this area is closed," I said. "Nobody else is sitting at any of the tables nearby, and there are no waiters. Maybe we should move."

"No way." He waved me off. "They'll bring our food. They love me here."

The way everyone in the place was frowning at us, I doubted there was much love. But Flynner was oblivious.

"Listen, football pays all the bills at Pinnacle. And Pinnacle pays all the bills in this lame town," Flynner said. "And I'm the reason the football

49

team is so famous and brings in so much money. So everyone loves me."

Before I could answer, a waitress appeared with a huge glass of Coke for Flynner. She glanced at me. "What can I get you, honey?"

"He'll have what I'm having," Flynner replied. "I'm his hero. Right, Hardy?"

He was teasing me, but I had to go along with it. "Right," I said.

"Well, you're everybody's hero," the waitress replied, turning away. I thought she was being sarcastic, but Flynner just grinned.

"It's terrible, what happened to Orena," I began.

"I guess. I barely knew him." Flynner sounded bored. He really was a jerk. Obviously it was time for a subject change. And I knew just what to talk about.

"So it seems like you're pretty up on all the money stuff, huh?" I asked innocently. "I mean, you were talking about Pinnacle football paying the bills. . . ."

"Listen to me, Hardy. You gotta know what you're worth," Flynner said seriously. "If all I knew was how to pass and how to scramble, I'd be a good quarterback. But that's not enough. I have to think long-term. I mean, even players like me have short careers. Professional football players are washed up by the time they're thirty-five."

"Maybe. But at least you'll get to play pro," I argued. "Some of us don't even stand a chance of doing that."

Flynner narrowed his eyes and studied me for a minute. I forced myself to take a sip of Coke as if everything was normal. But the way he was looking at me . . . Had I said something suspicious? I was only trying to make him talk money.

Finally Flynner grinned. "It doesn't matter if you can't go pro. You have to work with what you've got, Hardy."

"Okay," I said. "I'm a backup kicker on a college team. That's what I've got. I'm not like you. I'll never make it to the NFL."

"Then you have to do your thing while you're still in college." Flynner said. "You have to think big, Hardy. You have to understand the big picture."

"What's the big picture?" I asked.

"It's the business, man," said Flynner. "Football isn't about winning or losing. It's about making the dough for people when you win and making the dough for people when you lose."

"Who makes money when you lose?" I asked. This hero-worship thing was totally working. The

dude seemed ready to tell me anything I wanted to know. Under the table, I unhooked my ATAC music player/surveillance device and pressed the button to record.

"It's not people you know," Flynner explained. "I'm talking about a bunch of people, all over the country, who put money on you to win or to lose."

"You mean betting?" I asked. "Gambling?"

"Sure, betting. People put a huge amount of money on college games."

"I thought it was illegal in a lot of states," I said.

Flynner shrugged. "So what? Everybody does it. And if you know the people who are betting on you to lose, then you can help them out a little. For the right price."

"I don't get it," I said, playing dumb. I wanted a full confession from this loser.

"These high rollers, these guys with a ton of money, they like to make even more money," Flynner revealed, leaning across the table to me. "And say there's a team that is a sure thing to win—"

"Like Pinnacle," I put in.

"Right. So all kinds of people are putting their money on Pinnacle to win," said Flynner. "But say these high rollers know for sure that Pinnacle is going to *lose*. They bet against Pinnacle while everyone else bets for Pinnacle. Then when Pinnacle loses, the high rollers make a fortune."

"Okay," I said carefully.

Flynner rolled his eyes. "These high rollers are willing to pay players to make it happen," he said slowly, like he was talking to a two-year-old. "They have enough money, and they look at it as an investment."

"So they'll pay a football player to make sure his team loses," I summed up.

"Yeah." Flynner grinned. "And that's the big picture. Easy money. And even a loser like you can do it—you don't have to be NFL-bound like me."

"Well, *you* couldn't do that," I said. "I mean, you'd have to pretend to play badly. And then none of the NFL teams would want you."

"That's true," he agreed. "That's why I used the money to buy myself the best NFL draft spot."

"What?" I cried.

"Yeah. I have a friend who can pull strings. And he has some friends who want Pinnacle to lose the championship next week. They're willing to pay me to do it."

"But instead you told your friend to keep the

money in exchange for snagging you the top over-all draft spot," I guessed. "That's the slot that gets you the most money."

"Yup. You catch on fast, Hardy. See, now I'll definitely have my NFL career. *And* I'll know the high rollers. They bet on professional games too. And I guarantee they'll pay me a lot more to throw an NFL game than a college one." Flynner stopped talking while the waitress plopped a couple of cheeseburgers down in front of us. He waited until she walked away, then he looked me straight in the eye. "You want in?"

I almost choked on my first bite. "Me?"

"Yeah. You seem like a good kid. And I can't lose the whole game all by myself. You might be able to help me."

"I don't know," I said. "I'm only the backup. I won't even be playing."

"Yeah, well . . ." Flynner gave me a wink. "You never know what could happen between now and Saturday."

"I can't believe it," Frank said when I played him the tape later. "This guy is a huge idiot."

"I know." I glanced over my shoulder to make sure Luis and Ken weren't nearby. But the coast was clear—they were playing foosball in the common room and yelling the whole time. "He thinks he'll get away with being a crooked player in front of millions of people. As if nobody is ever gonna find out. He thinks it's a good plan to save money for when he has to retire!"

"If he just played well in the championship, he'd probably get drafted to some NFL team anyway," said Frank, shaking his head. "And then he'd make enough money to live on for a hundred years."

I shrugged. "He's greedy."

"He's stupid."

"Whatever," I replied. "He's the one. He admitted it, we have it on tape. Mission accomplished!"

Frank shoved my arm. "Now you're being stupid."

"Ow," I said.

"Flynner said it himself—he can't lose the entire game all alone. There have to be other players in on it. And besides, it wasn't his idea. That friend of his, the one with the inside track on the NFL draft. He's the middle man between Flynner and the high rollers. That's who we want. That's the mastermind."

I groaned. "I thought we were done."

"Is practice so hard that you can't stand another day of it?" Frank teased.

"No," I said. "Flynner is so obnoxious that I can't stand hanging out with him!"

"Well, you have to," Frank told me. "You've got to find out who he's working for."

6.

Playing by the Book

"Memorize the *entire* playbook," Coach Orman said on Wednesday after practice. "I don't mean only the plays that concern you and your position. I mean the whole thing."

I watched from the doorway of Coach's office as the team mumbled and groaned. I had to admit, memorizing an entire playbook three days before the final game of the year did seem a little harsh. But Coach Orman was all about discipline, and if he wanted them to do it, there must be a good reason.

"That's crazy," said Manzi from beside me. "They don't have time to do that."

I glanced at the other manager. He and I had done all the cleaning by ourselves during practice because John Roque was making sure the play-books all got printed correctly at the campus copy center.

"It's not crazy," I told Manzi. "Coach probably wants to make sure they're thinking about football twenty-four/seven. When they're not practicing, they're memorizing plays. It keeps them from getting distracted."

"I guess. He already banned them from seeing their girlfriends until after the game." Manzi chuckled. "You should've heard them complaining after that announcement. This is nothing compared to it."

Still, the players didn't look very happy. Between Orena's unexpected death, the pressure of the championship, and now the added homework, they were an angry bunch of guys. That was bad news for me. When they were mad, they threw their equipment and their towels all over the place, and I had to pick everything up and organize it.

"John is getting the playbooks ready, and he'll deliver them to your dorms in about an hour," Coach announced. "Hit the showers."

While I did the rounds, collecting all the dirty uniforms and dumping them into the laundry bin, I kept an eye on Anthony Aloia, the best receiver on the team. He was almost as big a star as Billy

Flynn, but their personalities couldn't be any more different. Flynner was always talking about himself. Loudly. And according to Joe, he didn't have a single ethical bone in his body.

But Anthony Aloia kept to himself. He didn't talk much in team meetings, from what I'd seen. And he didn't seem to have a posse on the team. He was a loner. But he seemed nice enough. He put his own uniform in the bin instead of leaving it on the floor for me to pick up. When he slammed his locker shut and turned to leave, I casually headed toward him.

"Hey. You're Anthony, right?" I asked. "I'm Frank Hardy. I'm the new manager."

"Hey, man," he said. "Welcome." Anthony headed for the door.

Uh-oh. I was supposed to get him to talk. Right now Joe was way ahead of me in breaking this case. I thought fast. "I'm a big fan of yours," I called after Anthony. Hero worship had worked for Joe. Maybe it would work for me, too.

"Thanks," he said, looking over his shoulder.

"Yeah, I think it's the receivers who really make the team," I told him. "No matter who your quarterback is, if you don't have a strong receiver, then there's no one to catch the ball."

He chuckled. I had him.

"So, listen, I'd be happy to help you out with this playbook thing," I offered. "If you want a hand memorizing it."

"Um . . . ," Anthony began.

"Seriously, I'm very good at memorization," I hurried on. "I tutor people, that's my part-time job. I know all kinds of tricks to help you remember stuff."

Anthony frowned. "Do you want me to pay you?"

"No!" I cried. "That's not what I meant. I just figured I could help."

"Okay," said Anthony. "When?"

I glanced around the locker room. All the other players were on their way out, and Manzi was mopping in the showers. "How about now?" I said. "I can call up the playbook on Coach's computer. He's gone already."

"Cool." Anthony followed me into the office and dropped onto the tiny couch. I sat at the desk and clicked on the playbook. Roque had left the file open. "Let's start with the halfback option—twin receiver set," I suggested.

"The quarterback reads the defense and decides whether to hand off to the halfback or to make a play downfield to one of the two receivers on the right side of the field," Anthony replied immediately.

"You're good," I said.

"Offensive plays I already know." He shrugged. "It's the defensive plays I'm not up on. Let's do those."

I scrolled through the file until I reached Defense, and we got down to it. As we worked, I kept an eye on Anthony to see if he could be hiding anything. But the whole time, he was all business. A total pro. I couldn't get him to talk about anything but football plays.

This is a complete failure, I thought, bummed. *I'm not getting any info at all out of him.*

"What's going on?" Roque's voice made me jump. He was standing in the doorway of Coach's office, and he was frowning.

"Oh, we're just—," I began.

"We're working on the playbook, what does it look like?" Anthony cut in. "Did you think you were the only one allowed in here?"

Wow, I thought. Anthony's tone was super cold all of a sudden.

"I didn't say that," replied Roque.

"Yeah, and you better not say it," Anthony snapped. "If I want to be in Coach's office, I can be. I actually score points for this team. What do *you* do, loser?"

"Hey, guys—," I started.

"It's okay. I'm gonna go." Roque spun away. "You lock up, Hardy." He hurried out, not even looking in Anthony's direction again.

I glanced at Anthony. He was staring at Roque's back as if he wanted to hurl a knife at it or something.

"What was that about?" I asked.

"Nothing." Anthony shrugged and turned back to me. "That dude just annoys me."

"Roque? How come?"

" 'Cause he's obnoxious. Why is he even here? He doesn't need a job. His dad is a gazillionaire." For the first time, Anthony sounded passionate about something. Passionately angry.

"But we don't get paid to be managers—"

"Still, why is he here? He's not a player. He's just a spoiled little rich kid."

"He, um, he told me he was trying to make his father happy. You know, since he's not a player. At least he can work for the team. . . ."

"Typical." Anthony snorted. "It's all about Daddy getting what he wants."

"Do you know Roque's father?" I asked. "Dr. Roque?"

"Of course. We all know him. He's a booster." Anthony shoved a hand through his hair. "He's at all the games. Every single team fund-raising event. I'm surprised he hasn't been coming to practice this week."

The way Anthony said the word "booster" made it sound like a huge insult.

"What's a booster?" I asked.

"A team booster. It's like a sponsor," explained Anthony. "People with more money than they know what to do with, so they spend it on the football team. They donate the cash to buy all our equipment and to pay the upkeep on the gym and the stadium and all." He gave a bitter laugh. "And they pay for scholarships. If you can play, they'll pay for your college. The whole thing."

"Sounds nice," I said.

"It's not. Guys like Dr. Roque are so full of themselves. He thinks he can throw money at anyone and get them to do whatever he wants."

Now that sounded interesting. "What do you mean?"

"Nothing." Anthony stood up and began to pace. "It's just . . . these boosters. They act as if they can buy anything. Even people. And they don't care who gets hurt because of it."

"Who's getting hurt?" I asked.

He stared at me for a second, then sat back down. "Never mind."

He had been about to say something important,

I knew it. So I decided to press. "It sounds like the boosters only help, not hurt. Think about it. The football team is doing great. The facilities are state-of-the-art. Players get full scholarships—"

"Yeah, well, what about Coach?" Anthony interrupted. "He's getting hurt."

"Coach Orman? How?" I asked.

"Everybody knows Dr. Roque has been trying to get Coach fired all year long. We've had an amazing season. We're top ranked! But Dr. Roque wants to lose the coach who got us here."

"Why?"

"Who knows? They hate each other. Every time Dr. Roque is at practice, he's always trying to tell Coach to do things differently. He even came down to the sidelines during one of the games, just to butt in." Anthony shook his head. "The guy's not a coach. He was a great player a million years ago, so what? Now he's just a rich dude. He should leave the coaching to Coach."

"But he doesn't get to decide, does he?" I asked. "Just because he hates Coach, that doesn't mean he can actually fire him."

"Try telling that to Dr. Roque," Anthony said. "He sure thinks it's up to him. That's what I'm talking about. He figures that because he buys stuff for the team, it's as if he owns the team."

"But he doesn't. He's just donating that money to the college."

"I know. Still, Dr. Roque has a ton of friends on the college board. The way I see it, it's only a matter of time before he gets his way and Coach Orman gets sacked."

The *Monday Night Football* theme rang through the air. "That's my cell," said Anthony. He pulled a beat-up old phone from his pocket and hit the Talk button. "Hey, what's up?"

I turned to the playbook on the computer, searching for the next play we hadn't covered. But I was keeping an eye on Anthony, too.

"What are you talking about?" he said, his voice agitated.

I eased my chair around so I could see him. His face had gone completely white.

"No!" he suddenly barked.

This time I turned all the way. Anthony was freaking out. Beads of sweat popped out on his forehead, and he was back on his feet. He seemed to have forgotten I was there, he was listening so intently to the person at the other end of the line.

"Fine," he said finally. He flipped the phone shut and gazed at it for a second.

"Hey, man, is everything okay?" I asked.

Anthony raised his eyes to mine. "I gotta go," he mumbled. He grabbed his gym bag and stalked out of the office without another word.

7.

All About the Money

I scanned the big reading room at the library. Every single person there was a football player. Of course, that was probably because it was winter break and most of the students were done with finals for the semester. The only reason anyone was still on campus was to see the upcoming championship game against Miller State.

"Hey, Hardy," Ken called from a table on the right.

"Hey." I wandered over. "I guess everybody's studying the playbook, huh?"

"Yeah. Hard to believe the library didn't fall down from the shock of all these jocks actually entering it." Ken grinned, and Luis laughed from across the table.

67

"So you're not usually big on the books?" I guessed.

"Are you kidding? Football players barely even have to pass," Luis told me. "The college board wants us here to play, not to work."

"Speak for yourself," said Ken. "Some of us also want good grades so we can have a future. You can't play football forever."

That's just what Flynner said, I thought. "You guys seen Flynner?" I asked.

They both looked at me strangely. "Yeah, he's in the back," Luis said. "What are you, his best friend now?"

"I'm just a fan," I told my suitemate. "Later."

I headed for the back of the reading room. Flynner sat at a table twenty feet away from everybody else. There was one guy with him. A glance at his face told me he was Marco Muñoz, the best running back on the team. I recognized his face from the ATAC dossier. Score. Frank and I had been meaning to investigate that dude.

"Hey," I said. "You mind if I sit here?"

"Yes," Marco replied.

But Flynner shoved his shoulder. "Don't be rude. Hardy's my boy. Right?"

"Uh, right," I forced myself to say.

"Sit. Study." Flynner grinned.

I sat a couple of chairs away from them and pulled out the printout of the playbook that John Roque had delivered to my dorm room. I had to admit, I was kind of surprised that Flynner was bothering to study the thing. He seemed like the kind of guy who wouldn't care at all what Coach told him to do. Especially since he was planning to lose the game.

Marco was shooting me dirty looks, and he and Flynner were both really quiet. I got the feeling I'd interrupted something. So I pulled out my ATAC music player and stuck the earbuds into my ears. That way, they would think they had privacy. They'd figure I was listening to music and couldn't hear them. Of course, what I was really doing was listening to *them*, using the superpowerful mike on the device.

Marco gave me another look, then shifted in his seat to move closer to Flynner. "What are you doing?" he muttered. "Who is this dude?"

"New backup kicker," replied Flynner.

"We were in the middle of a conversation," Marco hissed.

"He doesn't care," Flynner said, unconcerned. "He's not even paying attention."

"Fine. Whatever." Marco sounded furious. "So tell me how much."

"First tell me you're in," Flynner countered.

"No, I need to know a dollar amount. I'm not doing this for nothing. I have standards."

Flynner snorted. "Yeah? You're willing to throw a championship game and you think you have *standards*?"

"What are you talking about? You're willing to throw the game too," snapped Marco.

He glanced over at me. I kept my eyes on the playbook and my face blank. But inside I was doing a victory dance like a receiver in the end zone. I didn't even have to bother investigating Marco. He'd basically just admitted that he was in on it. These idiots were actually discussing their illegal plan right next to me!

"Yeah. But I'm not pretending to be all noble," Flynner said. "I'm in it to secure my future."

"Don't you even care how you're going to look?" asked Marco, frowning. "It's the last game of the season, and I'm gonna go out looking bad. What if Coach doesn't want to start me next season because of this game?"

"You don't have to be terrible," Flynner pointed out. "Just fumble a few times. Let yourself get tackled. It will look like you had an off day."

"But it's embarrassing," Marco said. "And it's

SUSPECT PROFILE

Name: Marco Muñoz

Hometown: Grand Rapids, Michigan

Physical description: 20 years old; 6'4", 198 lbs.;
dark hair and eyes.

Occupation: Junior at Pinnacle College; running back
for the Mountain Lions

Background: High school all-star; on a football
scholarship at Pinnacle.

Suspicious behavior: Discussed throwing the game
with Billy Flynn.

Suspected of: Conspiring to lose the championship
game.

Possible motive: Greed.

your last college game, *ever*. You're a senior. Doesn't
it bother you that thousands of people are going to
see you lose the game for Pinnacle?"

Flynner shrugged. "It's only one game. I have a
whole career ahead of me."

Marco was silent for a minute, his forehead
creased in concentration. But I knew he wasn't

trying to memorize plays. He was thinking about messing up at the big game. He obviously wasn't too sure about the whole thing. Flynner didn't seem bothered by the idea at all, but Marco was a different story.

Maybe I could use that. Maybe I could convince him to tell me who the mastermind of this whole plan was.

"Don't tell me you're having second thoughts," Flynner said. "You said I could count on you."

"You have to tell me how much we're talking about," replied Marco. "If it's not enough to cover my credit card bill, it's not worth it to me. My parents will kill me if they find out I racked up that kind of debt."

"How deep are you in?"

Marco glanced at me again. Then he scribbled something on the edge of his playbook copy and pushed it across the table to Flynner.

Flynner read it and laughed out loud. "What have you been buying, diamonds for your prissy little girlfriend?"

"Forget it," Marco grumbled.

"Nah, it's cool. My friend will pay you that much, no problem. You can wipe the whole thing out at once. We just have to clear it with him." Flynner pushed back his chair and stood up. "Eight o'clock in the weight room. Be there."

He clapped me on the shoulder as he walked off.

Eight o'clock in the weight room, I thought. *I'll definitely be there.*

8.

Paying for the Past

I hate driving my motorcycle slowly. It's made for speed! But I'd been following Anthony Aloia all the way from the Pinnacle campus. If I sped up right behind him, he'd notice me for sure. I'd been on enough ATAC missions to know that the first rule of following a suspect is to stay two cars behind at all times.

Anthony's car was a beat-up old Chevy, which kinda surprised me. Most of the other players had expensive wheels. Flynner's Hummer had to be worth at least fifty grand. But I had to admit, Anthony's car fit in pretty well with the neighborhood we were in right now. It was only a twenty-minute drive from Pinnacle, but the place had seen better days. The houses mostly looked like

74

they could use a paint job, and several of the front yards were overgrown with weeds. A few had just been paved over with concrete. Some mean-looking dogs barked at me from behind chain-link fences, and I couldn't help noticing that a lot of homes had bars on the windows.

Still, there were kids playing outside. It had the feel of a lower-income area, but not a dangerous one. Anthony pulled into the driveway of a corner house. The name on the mailbox was ALOIA.

Got it, I thought. *This is his parents' house. Probably where he grew up.*

I sped on by. Then I turned onto the next street and parked my bike. I jogged back toward Anthony's place. He must have already gone inside. I checked out the house. It looked good. In fact, it was the best-kept house on the whole block. The paint was clean, the roof seemed new, and the grass was neatly mown.

In the driveway, next to Anthony's car, was a sweet little Volvo convertible.

That's weird, I thought. *Anthony drives an old wreck, but his parents have a new car?* It wasn't the most expensive car in the world, but it still seemed out of place in this neighborhood. I glanced around, checking for witnesses, then I hurried across the lawn and crouched behind the bushes that grew under the big front window. I inched up until I could see inside. Anthony was about six inches away!

I hit the dirt.

Five seconds went by. Ten seconds.

Nobody came out.

Whew! He must not have seen me.

I decided not to push my luck. I stayed down under the window. But I pulled my ATAC surveillance device from my pocket. The earpiece doubled as a supersensitive microphone. I reached up and carefully pressed it against the glass. I stuck the other piece in my ear.

Perfection. I could hear everything as clearly as if I was in the room myself.

". . . ruining my life!" Anthony was yelling.

"Calm down, sweetheart," a woman said. Anthony's mother, I figured.

"No! I will not calm down," snapped Anthony. "You two have been telling me to calm down for two years now—"

"That's because there's nothing wrong," a man cut in. That had to be Anthony's dad. "You're always worrying about things that aren't important."

"Well, this is important," Anthony said. "I told you over and over that you weren't supposed to take gifts from that jerk. But you just ignored me.

You had to have your precious plasma TV and your nice car and your—"

"Why shouldn't we have nice things?" Anthony's mother cried. "We deserve them as much as anybody else!"

"I'm not saying you don't deserve them," replied Anthony.

"You know we can't afford this kind of stuff on our own," his father put in. "If Dr. Roque wants to give us things, why shouldn't we take them?"

"Because it's against the rules!" Anthony exploded. "This stuff was all a bribe to get me to go to Pinnacle instead of another school."

"Son, you didn't want to go to any other school," his mom observed. "You never wanted to go far from home."

"That's not the point," said Anthony. "The point is, Dr. Roque didn't know that. So he gave you all these expensive things to make sure you sent me to his college. That's all he cared about. It's not like he's your friend or something."

"We never thought he was," Mr. Aloia said. "But that's no reason not to take what he was offering—"

"It could get me thrown out of school," Anthony interrupted. "Because of you, I could get kicked off the football team."

His parents were both silent.

"The boosters aren't allowed to give personal gifts," Anthony went on. His voice was quieter now. "It's against the regulations that govern college football. I kept telling you that."

"But *you* didn't take any gifts," his mother protested.

"My family did. That's still against the rules. If the Ethics Board finds out, I'm done," said Anthony. "Pinnacle will kick me out, and no other college team will have me. And if I can't play college ball, you can forget about professional football. I'll never get into the NFL. I won't even have a chance."

"I don't understand," Anthony's father said. "Why are you so upset about this all of a sudden?"

"Listen." I heard Anthony moving around inside, so I risked another peek through the window. Anthony was punching the buttons of his cell phone. He set it down on the coffee table. "It's on speaker," he told his parents. "I've gotten three of these calls in the past hour. When I stopped answering my phone, he left a message."

He punched one more button on the phone, and his voice mail began to play.

A strange voice came over the line. It sounded almost like a computerized voice, flat and distorted. But there was something human and threatening in the tone, something a computer could never convey.

"Aloia. I know you took bribes from a booster. I have proof. And I'm willing to take it to the Ethics Board," the voice said.

Anthony's mother gasped.

"There is only one way to stop me," the voice went on. "You have to drop the ball on Saturday."

"What? What is that supposed to mean?" Mr. Aloia sounded frightened.

SUSPECT PROFILE

Name: Anthony Aloia

Hometown: Pinnacle Heights, Colorado

Physical description: 20 years old; 6'5", 206 lbs.; dark hair, blue eyes.

Occupation: Junior at Pinnacle College; receiver on the Mountain Lions

Background: Played football at public high school for two years; got a scholarship to a private high school for his final year.

Suspicious behavior: Overheard telling his parents he planned to throw the game.

Suspected of: Conspiring to lose the championship game.

Possible motive: Wants to protect his parents and his future in the sport.

"It means he wants me to throw the game," said Anthony. "And I have to do it."

I couldn't believe it. Anthony was being black-mailed!

9.

Conspiracy

"No one will hear us in here," I said, glancing around.

Sure enough, the laundry room in the dorm was totally empty. A lot of students had gone home for the winter break, and the football team probably didn't even care about having clean clothes.

Frank stuck a quarter into one of the dryers and turned it on. "Just in case," he said over the noise.

"Okay, so here's what we know. We know Flynner is definitely planning to lose the game," I stated.

"In return for the best NFL draft slot," Frank put in.

"And Marco is planning to help him, maybe. . . ."

"If Flynner's mysterious 'friend' coughs up enough dough," added Frank.

"And Anthony will also help, because he's got no choice. The so-called friend will ruin his whole football career if he doesn't." I frowned. "So we've got the quarterback, the star receiver, and the best running back."

"Everyone you really need," Frank summed up. "Those three guys score most of the points. Even if the defense manages to keep Miller State from scoring, Pinnacle still needs to put the ball in the end zone in order to win."

"Yeah. We've got everything we need to bring this ring down . . . except the person who's behind it." I leaned against one of the washing machines. "That's the one we need."

"But instead we keep finding everyone else," complained Frank. "We have to get these guys to tell us who's running the show. We only have three days."

I grinned. "No problem."

"What do you mean, no problem?"

"I'm on it," I told my brother.

Frank rolled his eyes. "What is that supposed to mean?"

"Look, I'm in good with Flynner. He thinks I'm like a little puppy dog who will follow him around and love him no matter what."

"Yeah, you're good at kissing butt," Frank joked.

"And I happen to know that Flynner and Marco are meeting in the weight room in about ten minutes. Flynner's supposed to tell Marco how much money he's gonna get." I shrugged. "So I'll be there."

"Huh?" asked Frank.

"I'll go to the weight room. They're talking about the 'friend.' They're talking about the plan to lose the game. They'll probably tell us everything we need to know."

"Sure. Except that if you're there, they won't be talking about any of it," Frank pointed out.

"Flynner doesn't care who finds out. He's an idiot," I said. "He told me straight to my face that he was gonna throw the game."

"But Marco cares." Frank paced around the small room. "You have to get him to trust you too."

"How?"

"Tell them you want in," he suggested. "I mean, Flynner asked you to help him. So you tell him yes."

"And if I do it in front of Marco, Marco will believe that I'm on their side," I said.

"Yup." Frank headed for the laundry room door. "You better get going. The weight room is on the other side of campus."

"Are you coming?"

"You know it. I'll listen in and see if there's anything worth recording." He patted the music player/surveillance device on his belt. "We can use the remote record feature."

"Cool!" Our ATAC devices had this awesome thing where we could connect to each other wirelessly, and still use the microphone and record functions. I'd just turn my device on, link to my brother, and talk to Flynner and Marco like everything was normal. But Frank would be eavesdropping though his device—and taping anything that sounded important.

"Let's go." I led the way out of the room and up the stairs from the dorm basement. "Maybe we'll get lucky. Maybe the ringleader will show up for this little meeting."

"I'll be happy if we just get his name," Frank said. "Then our mission will be over. I'm getting tired of mopping floors!"

Score! I thought when I shoved open the weight room door. Not only were Flynner and Marco inside, but Anthony was there too. *This looks like a meeting of the whole gang.* Now I just needed Flynner's influential friend to show up, and we'd be all set.

I was psyched.

The football players weren't.

"Hardy? What are *you* doing here?" Anthony cried. He looked nervous.

Marco spun around to face Flynner. "Did you invite this loser? You told me he wasn't even listening in the library!"

"I didn't invite him." Flynner walked over and pulled the door shut. "But it's no big deal."

"Hey, guys—," I started.

"It is too a big deal!" Anthony exploded. "I don't even want to be here! It's bad enough I have to do this thing. If anyone—*anyone*—finds out, I'll get kicked off the team. And that's what I'm trying to avoid!"

"He's right. We're in huge trouble if anybody catches us," Marco agreed. "And the more people who know, the better the chance that our secret will get out."

"Chill. Hardy's not a snitch," said Flynner. He lay down on the bench as if he were taking a relaxing nap.

"Did you tell him the whole plan?" cried Anthony. "Flynner, you moron!"

"You guys, seriously, calm down," I cut in. "I'm not gonna tell. I'm just here because I want in."

They all stared at me.

"You asked me if I wanted to help. I do," I told Flynner.

"I was kinda kidding," he replied.

"Well, I'm not," I said.

"Why?" Anthony looked at me like he wanted to punch me. "Why would anyone *want* to lose a championship on purpose?"

"Don't be such a goody-goody," Marco snapped. "Flynner and I are both here because we want to be. Maybe you should leave."

"Believe me, I want to," Anthony retorted, getting in Marco's face. "I think you guys are complete traitors."

"You're still here," Flynner pointed out.

Anthony backed down. "I have no choice. Your friend is blackmailing me."

Flynner shrugged. "Sorry, man. I offered you money to do it." He bench-pressed a three-hundred-pound weight, looking bored.

"I don't want money. I want to win the game," said Anthony.

"Well, it wasn't my idea to blackmail you," Flynner replied. "I don't even know what he's got on you. Is it anything good?"

"Shut up," Anthony muttered.

"I just want the money," I put in. They all looked at me again. I think they'd forgotten I was there. "I have my eye on a new motorcycle," I added.

Anthony shook his head, disgusted.

"Forget it," said Marco. "Why should our friend give you any money? You can't help us."

"I can miss a field-goal kick," I said. *Without even trying*, I added silently.

"You're just the backup kicker. You won't even get the chance to miss a field goal. You're not gonna be playing," Marco told me.

"And even if you were, why should we trust you?" Anthony asked. "You just got here, like, three days ago. We don't know anything about you."

Flynner stood up. "That's no problem. Hardy will just have to prove that he's trustworthy." He grinned at me. "You want in? You got it. But I'm not gonna bother my friend with this until you show us you're serious."

So much for finishing the mission tonight, I thought. "What do you want me to do?" I asked Flynner.

"If you're going to help us, you need to be able

to play. The only way that will happen is if Ken is out of commission," he said. "So you get rid of Ken before the game, and we'll cut you in on the deal."

10.

A New Suspect?

"Get rid of Ken? How?" I heard my brother ask.

I pressed the earpiece of my ATAC surveillance device tighter into my ear. I didn't want to miss a word of this. The locker room bench I sat on was pretty uncomfortable, so I stood up and began to pace.

"I don't care. You figure it out," Flynner replied.

I stepped closer to the door that led to the weight room. The reception was better there.

"Hey, Frank."

For a second I didn't register that somebody had said *my* name. As in, somebody who could see me. Somebody who was not through that closed door into the weight room.

Uh-oh.

I turned slowly to find John Roque staring at me, eyebrow raised questioningly. "Whatcha doing?" he asked.

I shrugged. "Listening to some tunes." I pulled the earbuds of my multifunctional music player from my ears.

Roque nodded. "Just hanging out in the locker room by yourself, chilling to music?" He sounded doubtful. "This late at night?"

"What are *you* doing here so late?" I asked.

He looked startled. "Oh. I just came by to get the playbook off Coach's computer. He wants to make some changes."

"Really? Now that's everybody's memorized it?" I asked.

"Well, that was more about discipline than about actually remembering the plays." Roque leaned against a row of lockers. "Coach is always tweaking the playbook before big games. And he wants it all in the computer, like, instantly. So I have to drop everything and input the new stuff."

"Why doesn't he just make the changes himself?" I asked.

"Are you kidding? The man barely even knows how to turn the computer on," Roque joked. "I think he's afraid of it."

I laughed. "So you have to be here all night?"

"Nah. I'm just gonna download it and work on it in my dorm room." Roque held up his tricked-out PDA. Sweet. I guess Dr. Roque's money could buy a lot of technology.

"I guess it's more comfortable there," I said.

"Yeah. Microwave popcorn and everything." Roque narrowed his eyes at me. "What about you? How come you're hanging out all alone here?"

I was hoping he'd forgotten about that, I thought. The last thing we needed was to make anyone involved with the team suspicious of us. "Oh, I'm just looking for Joe," I lied. "He was supposed to meet me for a study session, and of course he didn't. I figured he might be here."

"In the locker room?"

"In the weight room," I said. "He's a workout fiend. Especially when he's trying to avoid studying. I was just about to check in there when you walked in."

"Oh." Roque was still looking at me with a weird expression on his face. I didn't think he believed me . . . until the weight room door swung open, and Joe came out.

My brother stopped short when he saw Roque.

"Joe," I said quickly. "Did you think I wouldn't find you? You're so predictable." I gave him a *play along* look, hoping he'd understand.

"Um, yeah, I guess the weight room was a pretty stupid place to hide," Joe said slowly.

"Come on. We're supposed to be studying," I told him.

"What are you guys studying in the middle of winter break?" asked Roque.

"Math," Joe answered immediately. "I suck at math. And the only way Pinnacle would let me transfer in was if I promised to take a math placement test at the beginning of the new semester. If I fail, I'm out."

"So he can't fail. We have a whole study plan," I put in.

"Wow. I thought they went easier on the academics with football players," Roque said.

"Yeah, well, he's not that good a player," I told him.

Joe shot me a death stare, but he didn't argue. "Let's just go study," he said.

"See you guys later." Roque turned toward Coach's office, and we hurried to the locker room door.

As soon as we were out into the hall of the sports complex, I let out a breath. "That was close."

"Do you think he's onto us?" Joe asked.

"I doubt it. As far as he could see, I was listening to my music player and looking for you. And since you were really in there, it will seem like I was telling the truth."

"Okay, good. He's not suspicious," said Joe.

"No. But I am," I stated.

"That's only because you know for a fact that we're lying about who we are," Joe joked.

"Funny," I said. "I mean, I'm suspicious of him. Roque."

"Why?"

"Because it was strange. I mean, who goes to the deserted locker room at night?"

"Well, me and you. And Flynner and Marco and Anthony . . ."

"Yeah, and all of us are involved in something shady," I pointed out. "Or at least, we're involved in busting up the shady deal."

"So you think Roque is involved too?"

"He said he was there to do computer stuff for Coach Orman. But what if that was a lie?" I said. "I mean, he was acting a little weird. I thought it was because he was wondering what I was doing there. But what if it was really because he was afraid of me?"

"You mean, he thought you were onto *him*?"

"It could be."

"They never told me the name of their friend, you know," Joe pointed out. "What if it's John Roque?

What if the real reason he was there was because he was going in to meet with the guys he paid off?"

"So he could be the one we're looking for," I reasoned. "John Roque could be the mastermind."

SUSPECT PROFILE

<u>Name</u>: John Roque

<u>Hometown</u>: Pinnacle Heights, Colorado

<u>Physical description</u>: 19 years old; 6'3", 198 lbs.; sandy hair, green eyes.

<u>Occupation</u>: Junior at Pinnacle College; team manager for the Mountain Lions

<u>Background</u>: Attended private boarding school in Massachusetts; moved back to his hometown for college.

<u>Suspicious behavior</u>: Caught hanging out near a meeting of the conspirators; had no good excuse to be there.

<u>Suspected of</u>: Leading the conspiracy to lose the championship game.

<u>Possible motive</u>: Unknown.

11.
Superstition

As we approached the dorm, I found myself walking slower and slower.

"What's up with you?" Frank asked.

"I'm worried about Ken," I admitted. "What am I supposed to do? Flynner and those guys are expecting me to take him out before the game."

"Did they say how? John walked in around then and I didn't hear the rest," said Frank.

"No. Marco and Anthony will barely speak to me. And Flynner couldn't care less how I do it, as long as I do it." I ran my hand through my hair. "I don't think he'd care if I shoved poor Ken out a window. That dude is a real jerk."

"Well, you're not gonna shove Ken out a

window," Frank told me. "We'll have to think of something else."

"Can't we just prove that John Roque is behind the whole thing?" I asked. "Then I don't have to do anything to Ken."

"Who knows how long it will take to get more info on John?" Frank said. "We have to keep going on the Joe-as-traitor story line too. Just in case."

"Great. So now I have to make sure that one of the only offensive players who's willing to score is unable to play on Saturday." I stopped outside the door of Brazelton Hall. "Basically, I have to add to the problem that ATAC sent us to solve."

"Look, you just have to do something temporary," said Frank. "Make it seem like Ken can't play for a couple of days. Hopefully we'll solve the case by Saturday, and then Ken can play."

"I think Flynner is expecting me to put Ken on the disabled list," I said.

"You can't. That's assault."

"Obviously I'm not gonna hurt the guy." I rolled my eyes. "But other than being injured, how do you get the starting kicker not to play in a championship game?"

Frank thought for a minute. "Um . . . kidnap him?"

"Yeah, or give him the wrong directions to his own football stadium."

"I guess we could try to trick him somehow," Frank said. "But how?"

The answer was so obvious that I had to laugh. "We psych him out. He's the most superstitious guy on the planet. Come on."

I raced inside and grabbed the elevator just as it was closing. By the time we got to our floor, we had the whole plan worked out—Frank would have to get Ken and Luis out of their room somehow, and I'd sneak in.

"Who's up for hall races?" Frank called as soon as I opened the door to the suite.

Ken and Luis were in the common room, as usual. They both spun around quickly. "What kind of racing?" asked Luis.

"I'm thinking one lap of jogging, one lap of combat crawling, and one lap of walking on your hands," Frank replied.

The football players stared at him. "I can't walk on my hands," Ken said.

"Sweet. Then I'm in. I'll kick your butt." Luis jumped up off the couch and headed for the hallway. "I did gymnastics in high school."

My mouth was already open to make fun of him, but Ken beat me to it.

"Ooh, wait till I tell the rest of the team about *that*. Did you wear tights?"

"Shut up," Luis said. "You're just afraid to race me."

"Am not."

"Are too."

"From the elevator all the way to the end of the hall and then back," Frank instructed. "That's a lap. You touch the wall, then move on to the next lap."

"Go!" Luis yelled.

"Wait, no fair!" Ken took off after him.

The second they were out of the suite, I ran into the guys' room—and stopped. Where did you keep a lucky sweatband? Where did you keep any kind of sweatband?

I scanned the dressers. No sweatband.

I checked the bedside tables. No luck.

Where would it be if it were mine? I wondered. I dropped to my knees and peered under the bed. There were tons of socks, but no lucky sweatband.

Then I realized where it had to be.

I approached Ken's bed slowly. He wouldn't really be that ridiculous, would he?

I lifted his pillow off the bed. Sure enough, there was the sweatband, carefully tucked under his pillow like a tooth for the tooth fairy.

"Only one lap to go!" Frank yelled from out in the hallway.

That was a warning, I knew. I grabbed the sweatband and stuffed it into the pocket of my track pants. Then I rearranged the pillow so that it looked the way it did when I came in. I managed to make it out into the hall just in time to see Luis speeding down the home stretch on his hands while Ken was stuck all the way at the end, trying to get his balance in a handstand and toppling over every time.

"Yes!" Luis bellowed as he hit the wall with his foot. "I win! I rule!" He flipped himself over onto his feet.

"It doesn't count. You're a gymnast," muttered Ken. "I should've gotten a head start."

"Best two out of three?" Luis challenged him.

Ken thought about it for a second.

"Or are you scared?" Luis teased.

Frank and I laughed.

"I need my lucky sweatband," Ken decided. "Then I'll totally beat you."

Frank's eyes met mine. I nodded. I'd gotten the sweatband. But I hadn't been expecting Ken to find out quite so soon.

Still, there was no way to stop him. He charged right past me into his room and yanked the pillow off the bed.

I cringed, knowing what was coming.

"Where's my sweatband?" Ken bellowed.

"Huh?" Frank asked innocently, stepping into the room.

"What's going on?" asked Luis. He stuck his head through the door. "You wussing out?"

"My sweatband is gone! Where is it? It's gone!" He glanced at me, his eyes wide. "Did you see it?"

"What? No. I don't even know where you keep that thing," I said.

"You took it, right?" Ken asked.

My heart stopped for a second. Had he seen me somehow? I thought he was busy racing up and down the hall.

"You took it—you're messing with me. Right?" Ken asked again. "Luis put you up to it. Right?"

"Hey, leave me out of this," exclaimed Luis, coming back into the suite.

"I didn't take it," I said.

"Then what were you doing in the suite? You weren't watching the race until the end," Ken pointed out.

Oops. The dude's pretty observant, I thought.

"He was in the bathroom. Duh," Frank put in.

"Yeah," I agreed. "Sorry. I didn't see your sweat-band in there."

"Then where is it?" Ken was starting to sound hysterical. "I need it to play."

"Did it fall under the bed?" asked Luis.

"No," Ken cried, checking under there.

"Maybe it's in your laundry bag or something?" I suggested.

"No! I don't wash it," he replied.

"Gross," said Frank.

"He's afraid the luck will wash off," Luis explained.

"Did you put it in your gym bag?" I asked. "Maybe you took it with you to practice and left it in your locker."

"I never leave it anywhere. Never. I wear it to practice and back, and then it goes under my pillow. It never goes anywhere else." Ken looked like he might cry.

"Don't worry, man, I'm sure it will turn up," Frank said.

Ken stared at him in disbelief.

"Uh, that's not good enough," Luis murmured. "We're gonna have a major freakout on our hands here."

"I can't play." Ken sat on his bed and dropped his head into his hands. "That's it. I just can't play."

"What?" I cried. "That's crazy."

"No, it's not. It's the smart thing to do," Ken said. "The sweatband is gone. It's a sign."

"Here we go." Luis threw up his hands.

"My luck is off," Ken told him. "You know I can't play with no luck. I'm out of the game."

"But the game isn't until Saturday. We can get you a new sweatband before then," I argued. But secretly, I was thrilled. This was working exactly the way we wanted it to.

"I can't get a new one," said Ken. His voice had turned sort of flat and weirdly reasonable. "The luck is attached to that one."

"Still, it's only one thing," Luis pointed out. "You still have the rest of your lucky superstitions. We'll all make sure we step into the rooms the right way, and we'll eat the right food on the right days."

"Yeah, and you still have that lucky blue golf ball in your locker at the gym," Frank reminded him. "I make sure it's there every time I clean out the locker room."

"See? There's all kinds of luck around," I said soothingly. *Don't believe me*, I silently added. *Your luck is shot. There's no way you can play without your sweatband.*

"No. There's no way I can play without my

lucky sweatband," Ken stated. "I just can't put the team at risk that way. Tomorrow I'll go to Coach and tell him he's got to put you in instead of me." He clapped me on the back. "You have to play in the big game, Hardy. Get ready."

12.
Tricks

"Coach is gonna flip out when Ken talks to him," Joe said as we walked across campus to practice on Thursday morning. "There's no way he'll let me play instead."

"It doesn't matter," I told him. "As long as Flynner or Marco or Anthony hears about it, you're in. They told you to get rid of Ken and you did. Everybody knows he'll never play if he thinks he's got bad luck."

"Yeah, that's true. Ken's the most superstitious guy ever. Even if Coach tells him to play, he won't." Joe grimaced. "But Coach isn't gonna be happy. I bet he really abuses me at practice today. He knows I can't kick. He'll be all over me, just in case I really do have to play on Saturday."

"Yep." I couldn't help smiling at the thought. "It'll be bad."

"It's up to you now," said Joe. "You have to get the dirt on John Roque—and fast."

"I will. I know he keeps everything on his Sidekick."

"Well, that's great, Frank," Joe said sarcastically. "Too bad he keeps that thing with him all the time."

"Not all the time," I noted. "He hooks it up to Coach's computer when he's editing the playbook. And last night he downloaded the playbook to his PDA. Which means that this morning, he'll be uploading it from his PDA back to Coach's computer."

"O-kay," Joe said. "And that helps us how?"

"All I have to do is interrupt him while he's doing it, and he'll leave his Sidekick there to finish the upload. Then I can hack in."

"Fine. But how are you gonna get him far enough away?" asked my brother. "I can't exactly challenge him to a race in the hallway. He's not an ultracompetitive football player."

"No, he's a techie," I said. "He needs a techie challenge. So I wrote a little program of my own last night. . . ."

Joe groaned. "It's a nerd-off."

"And I'm gonna run it this morning," I went on. "The scoreboard on the field is controlled by its own computer in the field house. That's where I'm going."

"The scoreboard?" Joe asked, confused.

I just waved over my shoulder as I jogged off toward the field house. As a team manager, I had keys to pretty much every door in the entire sports complex. I unlocked the door and headed straight for the lonely little computer in the middle of all the big ride-on mowers and field chalking machines.

I pulled a DVD from my jacket pocket and inserted it in the drive. "Piece of cake," I said to myself as my program installed. I had put in some encryption just to make it harder to find later on. And of course I'd made sure nobody could trace the application to me.

Five minutes later I was out on the field gazing at my work: the humongous scoreboard at the end of the football field didn't have any numbers on it. Instead it just had words, scrolling over and over. MILLER STATE RULES!

"Nice," I said. When the guys on the team saw that, they'd lose it. They would be sure that this was some lame prank pulled by the enemy school's students.

I grinned. This was kinda fun. It actually would be a good prank for Miller State to pull.

When I got inside, the locker room was full of players suiting up. John Roque was in the coach's office, but he hadn't gotten started on uploading the new and improved playbook. He was busy watching Coach Orman fight with Ken. All I had to do was wait.

"Mission accomplished?" Joe murmured, coming up behind me.

"Yup, we're all set," I said.

"That's ridiculous!" Coach's voice sounded furious. He'd been arguing with Ken, but now he started yelling. Everyone in the locker room stopped to listen—and to watch through the big windows in the office.

"Here we go," said my brother, worried.

"Hey, Hardy, what's the deal?" Flynner asked Joe. The quarterback never even seemed to notice me.

"Ken can't play on Saturday," explained Joe. "He's telling Coach now."

". . . should bench you for the entire next season for this stunt!" Coach yelled.

Ken answered him, but his voice was too quiet to hear.

"Get out!" Coach pointed to the door. "Don't even bother coming to practice today."

"Wow. Looks like Ken is really out," Flynner said. He ruffled Joe's hair as if he were a five-year-old kid. "Nice."

"Hardy!" Coach bellowed. "Get in here!"

"I'm guessing he means me," Joe said. "Wish me luck." He headed for the office, dread on his face.

"Both Hardys!" added Coach.

Uh-oh. I followed my brother.

Coach was red-faced and angry, but his voice had gone down a decibel. "Roque, give us a minute," he said. John Roque shot me a questioning look, then went out and closed the door behind him.

"I thought you clowns were supposed to stop this team from self-destructing," Coach said angrily. "Isn't that why you're here?"

"But you never thought the players were really planning to throw the game," I pointed out.

"That was before my star kicker suddenly decided to skip the most important game of the year," Coach growled. "You listen, and you listen good. If there is anything—*anything*—going on with this team, I want you to find it. *Now*. I will not have my perfect season ruined just because you two are the most useless undercover agents ever."

"We're not the ones who are planning to—," Joe began.

"I don't want to hear it," snapped Coach. "You better not be thinking about anything but kicking, just in case I have to play you on Saturday. And you—" He stabbed a finger at me. "You better make sure I don't have to play him on Saturday. Find out what's happening. And put an end to it. That's why you're here."

Coach yanked open the door and yelled into the locker room. "Get on the field! Twenty laps!"

Joe shot me a panicked look, then took off with the rest of the players. Coach stomped after them, along with his two assistant coaches.

"What was that all about?" John Roque asked, coming back into the office.

"Yeah, how come Coach wanted you?" said Manzi from behind him.

"My brother has to start on Saturday. Coach wants me to make sure he's psyched up for it," I lied. "He's worried because Joe is so green."

"I can't believe your brother is gonna get to play." Manzi shook his head as he headed over to the Gatorade cart. It was his turn to bring it out to the field for practice. "Some guys have all the luck."

"It is pretty fantastic." Roque plopped himself

down at Coach's desk and plugged his Sidekick into the computer. I could tell he didn't care at all about whether Joe got to play. Manzi had sounded jealous. Roque just sounded bored. The dude seriously didn't care about football.

Suddenly the walkie-talkie on Coach's desk crackled to life. "Roque! On the field, *stat*!" the coach's voice demanded.

Roque jumped in surprise. Coach almost never needed us during practice. As long as one manager was out there to take care of things, the other two were supposed to handle the inside duties. Roque grabbed the walkie-talkie. "What's up?" he asked.

"Some Miller State joker messed with the scoreboard. Get out here and fix it—now." Coach sounded like he couldn't believe his bad day.

I stifled a smile. "The scoreboard?"

Roque was already walking toward the door. "It's easy to rig if you know anything about computers," he said. "I'll be back in ten."

The instant he was gone, I turned to the desk. Sure enough, Roque's Sidekick was sitting there, still hooked to Coach's CPU. Finally we were catching a break in our investigation. I stopped the upload of the playbook, then I used the computer's keyboard and monitor to call up the directory for Roque's Sidekick. First I checked to see what kinds of software he had on the thing.

It was pretty tricked out. He had a ton of games, some that looked as if he'd written them himself. And he had the usual media storage programs for music and video. Tucked away in the middle of the list was an icon I didn't recognize, a big cartoon mouth. I clicked on it and opened the properties menu.

It was an audio program, and it seemed to modify the PDA's speakerphone. According to the menu, the application was called Voice. Under the "Author" category, it just said "Custom." I whistled. Roque certainly did a lot of programming on his own. He was a pretty serious computer geek. I opened the application, then dialed my own cell number. When my phone picked up, I spoke into the microphone of Roque's Sidekick.

I almost dropped both phones when I heard my voice on the other end.

It sounded flat, and deep, and strange.

It sounded like the voice I had heard on Anthony's voice mail message. The one from his black-mailer.

"Strike one for John Roque," I said, hanging up.

Next I opened up his document folder. I quickly scanned the files—the typical mix of e-mails, contact

111

lists, and text message conversations. And one really big spreadsheet. I clicked on it, and it opened up on Coach's monitor.

At the top was a title: "Miller State vs. Pinnacle." And in the columns were lists of names and numbers. There was no other information. But the numbers column had a header with a dollar sign on it. Between that and the title of the spreadsheet, it was pretty obvious. The names were people who had placed bets on the championship game. The numbers were the dollar amounts that they'd placed.

John Roque was a bookie.

He was in the business of gambling, taking the money of everybody who placed a bet with him and lost.

"Strike two, illegal gambling," I said out loud. Betting on college football was against the law in this state. "And strike three, conflict of interest." Roque was an official member of the Pinnacle Mountain Lions team, just like I was. He had insider information. Placing bets on the team, or against them, was basically like insider trading.

"Gotcha," I told the computer screen. I'd found our mastermind. I quickly stuck a memory card into Roque's Sidekick and copied the file. Just before I closed it, I scrolled down the massive list of names. He had a ton of clients. Obviously he'd been doing this bookie thing for a long time. The bets were mostly for a decent amount, with a few in the hundreds and most in the thousands.

And one for $250,000.

Wait, I thought. *That can't be right. Who would risk that kind of money on a football game?*

I ran my finger across the screen until I got to the names column.

Dr. Fred Roque.

My mouth dropped open. Dr. Roque was putting a huge amount of dough on the game. Dr. Roque, who had been trying all year to get Coach Orman fired. Dr. Roque, who had inside knowledge of the team through his son.

What better way to get rid of the coach than to make it look as if he'd choked in the most important game of the year?

Everyone in town, everyone on campus, practically everyone in the whole state had an interest in this game. If Pinnacle lost, the boosters would be crushed. They'd be angry. They'd want someone to blame. And the easiest person to blame was Coach Orman.

Dr. Roque's an ex-football player, so he has a lot of friends in the NFL, I thought. The pieces were all coming together. *He can pull strings to get Flynner his* top draft slot. *And he's got the money to buy off Marco. And he knows that Anthony's parents took a bribe, because he was the one who bribed them!*

Still, it was an expensive way to get rid of Coach Orman.

Dr. Roque must really hate the guy, like Anthony said, I thought. *But it doesn't hurt that he knows the team is going to lose, so he feels safe betting against them.* With $250,000 down, he'd probably end up making a huge amount of money on the deal even after paying off his crooked players.

I heard the locker room door open. Lightning fast, I yanked my memory card out of Roque's PDA and closed the file. Behind it, the playbook was still up on the monitor. I hit the button to resume upload, then I sprinted for the door.

Roque came around the last row of lockers to find me wiping down the bench.

"Did you fix the scoreboard?" I asked.

"Of course. Nothing to it." He grinned. "How's it going here?"

"Better than ever," I said. And I meant it.

SUSPECT PROFILE

Name: Dr. Fred Roque

Hometown: Pinnacle Heights, Colorado

Physical description: 45 years old; 6'5",
242 lbs.; sandy hair, blue eyes.

Occupation: Orthopedic surgeon; alumni
booster for the Mountain Lions

Background: Star quarterback at Pinnacle
College; played in the NFL until his career
was ended by an injury. Went to medical
school after leaving football.

Suspicious behavior: Placed large bet on the
championship game.

Suspected of: Planning the conspiracy to lose
the big game.

Possible motives: Wants to get Coach Orman
fired; greed.

13.

Fumble!

"My feet hurt," I complained on Friday morning.

"I know." Frank's voice came through the speaker in my motorcycle helmet. "You've said that five times already."

I pulled my bike up next to his as we rode along the two-lane mountain road. "My legs hurt too," I added. "And my back. Even my butt hurts."

"I don't feel sorry for you," my loving big brother replied. "You're getting to kick field goals in a famous college stadium with one of the best college football teams around."

"They're not real field goals, they're just practice," I said. "And I missed ninety percent of them. The whole team hates me."

"Look at it this way, they hate Ken more for

116

being so superstitious that he won't play," Frank pointed out. "And Flynner, Marco, and Anthony are totally on your side. If you were really planning to help lose the game, you wouldn't even have to try!"

"Shut up," I said. "Besides, Anthony hates me more than ever. He really doesn't want to throw the game. I think he hates all three of us for doing it on purpose. And Marco had another freak-out after practice yesterday. He's worried he's gonna look so bad that all the professional scouts will write him off."

"Don't worry, it's almost over," Frank told me. "As soon as we're done with Dr. Roque, you'll give Ken back his sweatband and the rest of the team will forget about the whole thing. Anthony will be off the hook, and so will Marco, as long as he didn't take any money yet."

"Yeah, but Flynner's the best quarterback in the league. There's no way he'll be allowed to play—he's been actively recruiting teammates to engage in illegal activity."

"True," said Frank. "But Luis is a great backup quarterback. The Mountain Lions could still pull it off. As long as they don't have to rely on you."

"Thanks," I muttered. "You know, my feet *really* hurt."

"Here's the turn." Frank leaned to the right, easing his motorcycle onto a small, winding road. Well, it looked like a road. But it was really a driveway—a half-mile-long driveway leading through Dr. Roque's land and right up to his humongous mansion.

We parked our bikes and checked the place out. Frank let out a low whistle.

"Maybe we should go into orthopedic surgery," I said.

"To get this kind of money, you have to have the professional football career first," Frank told me. "Even though Dr. Roque only played for five years before he broke his ankle, he made millions."

"Okay. I'll put that on my list of things to do," I joked. "Become NFL superstar. But not as a kicker."

Frank walked up the marble steps to the big front door. He rang the bell.

After a minute, the door opened, and there stood Fred Roque.

"Oh, Dr. Roque," I said, surprised. "I, um, I didn't expect you to answer the door yourself."

The huge guy chuckled. "I suppose I could hire somebody to do it. Just never occurred to me." He looked us up and down, smiling the whole time. "What can I do for you boys? Nice bikes," he added, glancing over our shoulders.

"Thanks," said Frank. "Zero to a hundred in three seconds."

"No way." Dr. Roque sounded impressed. And friendly. And cool.

We're here to bring this loser down, I reminded myself.

"I'm Joe Hardy, and this is my brother, Frank," I said. "We're on the football team at Pinnacle."

Dr. Roque's eyebrows knitted together. "You are? I don't recognize you. I know everyone on the team."

"We're new," Frank explained. "Brand-new. I'm a manager and Joe is the relief kicker."

Dr. Roque's eyes bored into me. "Is it true what I hear about Ken bailing out of the game tomorrow?" he demanded.

"Did John tell you about that?" I asked.

"John? No." Dr. Roque looked confused. "I spoke to McWilliams, the offensive coordinator. We're golf buddies. He keeps me informed."

I glanced at Frank. He shrugged.

"Yeah, it's true," I told Dr. Roque. "I made sure Ken wouldn't play tomorrow. Just like Flynner wanted me to."

"Huh?" he asked.

"I'm one of your boys, Dr. Roque," I said.

He stared at me for a second, then at Frank. Then he shrugged his broad shoulders. "Okay, I give up. What are you talking about?"

"Maybe we should come inside," suggested Frank.

"Sure." Dr. Roque opened the door wider, and we stepped into a massive, two-story-high atrium. "We can talk in my study." He led us across the big entryway and into a smaller, wood-paneled room off to the right. Football trophies lined the shelves next to the fireplace, and framed photos of the doctor with all kinds of famous football players hung on the walls.

Dr. Roque took a seat behind a supersized desk, and Frank and I sat in the two leather chairs across from him.

"All right now, Joe and Frank Hardy, tell me what you're talking about," Dr. Roque said. "Ken is refusing to kick, and you say it's your fault?" He frowned at me.

"Flynner told me that I couldn't join up unless I proved my loyalty. He wanted me to get rid of Ken, and I did. That way, I can play—badly—in the game tomorrow. And now you know that I'm no snitch."

Dr. Roque's mouth hung open. I had to hand it to the guy, he wasn't giving up easily. "Flynner . . . but why would you want to play badly?" he finally asked.

"To make the team lose. You're not gonna get your money otherwise," Frank said. "I saw your name on the list. You bet a quarter of a million dollars on this game."

That did it. Dr. Roque's face crumbled. "Oh, no. Are you cops?"

"We're part of an agency that works with the police," I said. "We could bring you down just for placing that bet. Gambling is illegal—"

"I know!" he wailed. "I know, I know, I know. I'm sorry. I knew it was wrong, and I've never done it before, you have to believe me."

Frank shot me a surprised look. Neither one of us was expecting the guy to go all apologetic like this. Criminals usually don't say they're sorry.

"I feel like such a hypocrite. I hate gambling! I do everything I can to fight it," Dr. Roque said miserably. "It's just that these guys at the club were talking last week, saying they'd heard the Mountain Lions were going to lose. Like it was an inside tip they had. I couldn't help myself. I had to stand up for my team. And then one thing led to another, and my pal from the club knew a bookie . . . and he dared me to put my money where my mouth was. . . ."

"Wait a minute," I said. "Are you telling us that you bet *on* the Mountain Lions? You bet that we would win?"

Dr. Roque blinked in surprise. "Yes. Of course."

"So you'll lose money if we lose," I stated.

"But that doesn't make sense," Frank put in. "If the team wins, you won't be able to get Coach Orman fired."

"Well, maybe not," said Dr. Roque. "I don't see what that has to do with it."

"We know you've been trying to get rid of him," I said.

"I have," he admitted. "Orman and I go way back. We played on the same team in college. I didn't like him then, and I don't like him now. I've registered my complaints with the Pinnacle board. Apart from that, there's nothing I can do."

My head was spinning. Frank looked as confused as I felt.

"So you bet on the team to win. And did you say that you don't even know the bookie?" Frank asked.

Dr. Roque shook his head. "I just called a number and got an electronic voice. Why? Is that who you're looking for, the bookie?"

"We're looking for the mastermind behind the plan to throw the game," I said. "And you were the one with the best motive. Or so we thought."

"Throw the game? As in, lose on purpose? The Mountain Lions?" All the color drained from Dr. Roque's face. "And Flynner is in on it, is that what you're saying?"

He didn't even seem to realize that we were accusing him of something. The guy was wigging out about the idea of losing.

"I knew that kid was no good." Dr. Roque slammed a beefy fist on his desk. "Who knows about this? How are we going to stop it? Wait, didn't you tell me you're in on it?"

This guy was big. Really big. Even though he'd been a quarterback, he was the size of a linebacker. I didn't want him going against me. "I'm pretending to be in on it," I said quickly. "Until we find out who's running the whole thing."

"What can I do?" he asked.

Frank and I looked at each other helplessly. "We're on it, Dr. Roque," my brother said. "We always accomplish our mission."

He sounded way more confident than I felt. How were we supposed to accomplish anything when our top suspect had turned out to be innocent?

We didn't have our guy.

And the game was tomorrow.

14.
Game Day

"It's John Roque," Joe insisted on Saturday morning. "That's who we thought it was before we found his father's name on the list."

"No, it's not," I told him for the tenth time. "John is a bookie. That's all. The voice modulator I found is to answer calls from his clients—remember, Dr. Roque said he got an electronic voice on the phone. Gambling is illegal. John's just trying to cover himself."

"We should still call the cops on him," muttered Joe. "He's committing a crime."

"Yeah. But not the crime we're here to stop," I said. "We can deal with Roque after we actually finish our own mission."

"And how are we gonna do that?" Joe asked.

"We still have no idea who's pulling the strings. And the game starts in two hours."

I sighed. "I think we have to punt."

"Ha-ha," Joe said sarcastically. "Football humor isn't very funny right now."

"I mean, I think we have to stop trying to figure out who Flynner's so-called friend is. We have to just ask outright."

"Are you kidding? We can't even get to Flynner," said Joe. "He's busy doing press. He had interviews starting at five o'clock this morning. All the papers want a quote from the hottest quarterback in college football."

"I can't wait to see what the articles actually say after everybody sees him play today," I remarked. "But we don't need Flynner. Marco is afraid of looking bad. And Anthony doesn't want to throw the game at all. We have to get one of them to tell us who it is."

"I don't think Anthony knows," Joe said.

"It's still worth a shot," I told him. "He must have some idea who would have the goods on him."

"All right. I'll try Marco," Joe decided. "I'll see you in the locker room." He grabbed his jacket off the bunk bed and stalked out of the room.

I put on my own coat and went out into the

common room. Luis had already left for the stadium, but Ken was sitting on the couch watching the pregame show on the local news. "Aren't you going to the game?" I asked. "Coach wants all the players there an hour and a half before kickoff."

"I don't know," said Ken. "I'm trying to figure out if my bad luck will rub off just because I'm there, even if I stay on the bench."

"The bad luck is in your head," I told him. "And Coach will kick you off the team for good if you don't show."

"I guess. I'll head over in a few." Ken turned back to the TV.

I caught a shuttle bus over to the stadium. The school was running them every fifteen minutes all day. Even so, I barely made it on because the thing was so packed. Everywhere I looked, people were dressed in black and gold, Pinnacle's colors. They had Mountain Lions flags, Mountain Lions jerseys, Mountain Lions caps. Some of them even had their faces painted like lions. This whole place had a serious case of Mountain Lion fever.

And their team was going to lose.

I had a sick feeling in my stomach as I listened to the other shuttle passengers sing the Pinnacle College fight song. They were all so happy, and their day was going to be ruined. All because Joe and I couldn't figure out who was planning to throw the game.

Maybe we should just call the cops on the three guys we know about, I thought. But I knew it wouldn't help. We had no proof that any of them were involved. They hadn't even done anything yet!

The shuttle bus jerked to a stop outside the entrance to the football stadium, and everyone piled off. The place was a madhouse. Campus workers were selling Pinnacle merchandise at little booths all over, thousands of fans were tailgating in the parking lot, and news crews roamed around interviewing people.

I pulled my team pass out of my pocket and looped it over my neck. I hadn't really needed it all week, but it was obvious that nobody without a pass would get near the locker room today.

The sports complex was banned to the public, but it was still crowded. More reporters were inside, and the players milled around talking to them.

As soon as the beefy security guys waved me past, I spotted Anthony Aloia. He was standing with his parents outside the locker room, giving a statement to a blond lady with a microphone. His parents were on camera too, but they didn't look very happy about it. Mrs. Aloia wore a fixed smile on her face, and Mr. Aloia glanced about nervously.

I stopped nearby and waited for him to finish.

"And that's junior sensation Anthony Aloia, getting ready for the big game," the reporter said, turning to the camera. Her camera guy nodded and turned off the camera, and she shook hands with the Aloias.

As soon as the woman turned away, Anthony ran a hand across his forehead. "I can't take this," he said quietly to his parents.

"You're doing fine, sweetheart," his mother replied. "Let's get you to the locker room. You'll feel better away from the press."

"I doubt it." Anthony sighed. "I just want to get this whole thing over with."

I hurried over before they could go anywhere. "Anthony! I need to talk to you," I said. "Now."

He looked surprised. "Uh, Mom and Dad, this is one of our team managers. . . ."

"Frank Hardy," I told them. "And I know what you're planning to do today."

All three of them stared at me for a second. Then Anthony shook his head. "Your brother told you. His brother is in on it," he explained to his mom and dad.

"No, he's not," I said. "Not really. Look, I know you're being blackmailed. All of you."

"What?" Mr. Aloia cried.

"You took a bribe from Dr. Roque—"

"We didn't know it was a bribe," Anthony's mom interrupted. "We thought they were just gifts. We'll give them back! We would do anything to help save our son's football career. . . ."

"Mom, it's too late." Anthony sounded resigned.

"Not if you tell me who's in charge of this whole thing," I said. "Joe and I are trying to figure out who's behind the conspiracy."

"So you want me to be a snitch. Flynner wants me to throw the game. How am I supposed to know what to do?" Anthony snapped.

"Honey, if you help bring down the guy who's responsible, maybe you won't have to play badly at all," said Mrs. Aloia. "Maybe the blackmailer will be arrested and we'll be off the hook!"

"Just tell me who this friend of Flynner's is," I said. "I promise Joe and I will do everything we can to help you out."

"I wish I could," Anthony told me. "I never met the guy. Believe me, I've been trying to figure out who it is. I just get these weird phone calls where the voice is disguised. Flynner is the only one who knows how to contact the dude, and he's always real careful not to say any names. To be honest, I'm not sure Flynner even knows who it is."

"I thought they were friends."

Anthony shrugged. "Flynner lies."

The assistant coach strode down the hallway, blowing his whistle. "Players inside!" he yelled. "Now!"

"Sorry I can't help," said Anthony. He gave his parents a sad smile. "See you after." He trudged off to the locker room.

As I headed after him, I spotted Coach Orman coming in the door at the end of the hall. Immediately he was mobbed by reporters. They all stuck microphones in his face, shouting questions at him.

Coach waved them off good-naturedly, pushing his way through them toward the locker room.

"Come on, just give us a prediction!" one of the reporters yelled.

"Catch me after the game, Trey," Coach called back. "I've got a big announcement for you."

He strode into the locker room, and the security guard moved to block the door.

"Hold on!" I called, waving my team pass. I stepped past the guard and followed Coach inside as the press swarmed the door behind us.

As soon as the players saw Coach Orman, they burst out cheering and whistling and yelling. The energy in the room was unreal—I'd never seen so many guys so psyched before. Even when Coach motioned for quiet, the cheering continued.

"We're number one!" Luis bellowed from ten feet away. One of the linebackers chest-bumped him in agreement.

Joe came over to me. "They think they're gonna win for sure," he said.

"I know." I stood on tiptoe to get a look around the humongous dudes standing in front of me. There, next to Coach, stood Flynner. He was grinning and high-fiving people just like everything was normal. But he was planning to betray everyone on the team.

"Did you talk to Marco?" I asked my brother.

"Yeah. He says he has no idea who Flynner's friend is." Joe shook his head. "Flynner won't tell. Marco said he asked point-blank, and Flynner refused to give him a name."

"Did you blow your cover?"

"Nah. I told him I wanted the name so that I'd know who to ask for my money after I missed a field goal or two."

"What did he say?"

"He laughed at me for being such an idiot. Said he'd told Flynner that the money had to be in his hands before the game or he wouldn't do it."

"So he got his money?" I asked.

"Yup. It was in his locker. And now it's like he doesn't even care anymore if he looks bad to the scouts. He must've gotten a lot of cash."

"All right, everyone, quiet down!" Coach yelled over the noise. "Now let's get serious. Today is our chance to prove to the world that we are as good as we say we are. Today is our chance to engrave this legendary team in the memory of Pinnacle College forever. Today is our chance to dominate!"

The Mountain Lions erupted in applause.

I felt sick. The game was going to start in less than an hour.

And we had nothing.

15.

Dropping the Ball

"M-O-U-N-T-A-I-N!" the head cheerleader yelled at the top of her lungs.

"L-I-O-N-S!" her partner bellowed.

"Mountain! Lions!"

Roooooooaaaaarrrrr!

The sound went up from all over the stadium, everybody in the crowd screaming the team's chant the way they did for each game Pinnacle played.

Except usually when the crowd roared, the Mountain Lions were winning.

"This sucks," Luis muttered from beside me on the bench. "How can they still be cheering like that? We look terrible out there."

"It's only the first quarter," I told him. "There's plenty of time."

"Hardy, they scored on the *first drive*," he said. "That was supposed to be our touchdown. We always come out throwing for the end zone, and we always make it. But Flynner threw an interception!"

"Well, all quarterbacks get picked off sometimes," I said lamely.

Luis shook his head. "Not Flynner. And that was hardly a pickoff. He threw it straight to the guy."

"Maybe all the media attention went to his head," said the dude next to Luis on the other side. "Flynner had about thirty interviewers telling him how great he was all morning."

"He *is* great," Luis said. He sounded like he was trying to convince himself. "He just has to get into a groove."

"He's not the only one," the other player muttered under his breath. "Aloia's dropped two perfectly good passes already."

"We're all nervous," I said. "The whole country is watching this game on TV." But my words sounded hollow, even to me. The fact was, Flynner was lobbing balls without even checking to see if there was a receiver open. At least Anthony had made it look like he was trying to catch the passes he dropped. The only bright side was that with the offense playing so badly, the defense got more time on the field.

None of them were trying to throw the game.

But it hardly mattered. Defense had never been Pinnacle's strong suit. The guys did their best, but Miller State was a powerhouse. Before the first quarter was over, they were up 14–0.

Most of the players on the bench sat with their heads in their hands. Even the crowd seemed depressed. Pinnacle had never looked so bad.

There were only twenty seconds to go in the quarter when Flynner handed off to Marco on a third down. Marco ran a few yards, then fumbled, the same way he had three times already. But just as a groan went up from thousands of people in the stands, one of the other running backs dove in and grabbed the ball in midair.

It was a catch!

He took off running for the end zone, leaving Marco in his dust. The Miller State defense rushed after him, but the Pinnacle blockers did their jobs. He ran to the fifty . . . the forty . . . the thirty-five . . . and a Miller State dude came out of nowhere to take him down.

We were all on our feet screaming encouragement. It was so amazing to see a great play from the Mountain Lions that I didn't even realize what was coming.

"Hardy!" Coach yelled. "Get in there."

What?

I looked at the scoreboard. It was a first down, but there were only eight seconds left. We were in field goal range.

The kicker was supposed to get out there and score.

All the blood drained from my face. I couldn't kick a field goal from that far, with thousands of people watching. I'd miss. I'd miss just like I had almost every time in practice for the last two days.

Pinnacle needed to score. The team couldn't take it if they went a whole quarter without putting points on the board. The other guys would get depressed and start to play sloppy, and then Flynner and his gang would hardly even have to try to lose the game.

I didn't even think. I just yanked Ken's lucky sweatband out of the handwarmer around my waist and thrust it at him.

Ken stared at me, astonished.

"I found your sweatband," I said. "Go score."

Ken shoved the thing onto his wrist, pulled on

his helmet, and ran onto the field. The guys on the bench sent up a huge cheer. Coach looked shocked.

But Flynner's mouth dropped open. He spun around and jabbed his finger at me accusingly.

I turned my back on him.

Ken was like poetry in motion. One smooth, fluid run toward the ball. A kick that looked as gentle as a love tap—but that thing *flew*! Straight through the goalposts.

The refs' arms shot up.

Field goal!

The crowd went nuts. So did the players. Everyone was so busy hugging and bumping chests that you would've thought we'd just won the game instead of putting up three lousy points.

It was such mayhem that it was hard to get anywhere near Ken as he jogged back over. Guys were shoving him and smacking him and head-butting him in congratulations. When Flynner stepped up, I figured he was gonna put on a show of being happy.

Instead, he put both hands on Ken's chest and shoved him—hard. Ken fell backward, his left leg clipping the edge of an equipment cart. He hit the ground.

Everyone gasped.

"Sorry, man," Flynner said casually. "I didn't see the cart there."

He was lying. It was so obvious. But nobody paid any attention to him, because they were all busy rushing over to Ken. My suitemate was clutching his leg where he'd hit the cart.

"Get the doctor!" shouted Coach.

The team doctor pushed through the press of players and knelt by Ken's side. He gently moved Ken's ankle to the left. Then to the right . . . and Ken cried out in pain.

"It's not broken, but it's a bad sprain," the doctor told Coach. "He's out for the game."

FRANK

"Let me see your pass," the security guard said, bored.

I held up the team badge, and he peered at it. "Fine." He leaned back against the wall and I went on into the sports complex. The place was deserted, especially compared to how crowded it had been earlier. Most of the reporters were in the stands watching the game.

A few small groups of people stood around, talking. I pushed the Gatorade cart past a woman talking into a camera. I didn't hear what she was saying, but the expression on her face said it all. The Mountain Lions were choking. The game had been a disaster so far.

". . . kicker is out for good," someone else was saying as I got closer to the locker room door. I slowed down to listen. "Word is that he's got a sprained ankle. He's elected to stay out on the field to support his teammates, but he'll be supporting them from the sidelines only."

I glanced over at the guy—and stopped. It was the same reporter that Coach had spoken to right before he went into the locker room before the game.

"This is Trey Beck with your game update. We'll check back at the half," he said, smiling like a big cheeseball.

"And . . . cut," the camera guy said.

Trey Beck dropped the stupid smile and loosened his tie.

"Excuse me," I called. "Mr. Beck?"

"Mm-hmm?" he replied, handing his mike off to the cameraman.

"I saw you earlier, talking to Coach Orman," I said. "He told you he was going to make an announcement after the game."

"Right," said the reporter.

"Do you know what it's about?" I asked.

"The announcement? The way things are going right now, it's going to be about the fact that his team lost their mojo," Trey joked. Then he noticed my badge and the Gatorade cart. "No offense," he added.

"None taken. I'm hoping they'll turn things around."

"Me too, kid. I've got a ton of money on this game." He yawned. "Anyway, I think Orman was planning to announce his retirement."

"Retirement?" I repeated. "But . . . but Coach isn't that old. Is he?"

"I guess he's kind of young for it," Trey agreed. "But that's the rumor in the press room." He popped a stick of gum into his mouth and wandered off down the hall.

I pulled open the locker room door and dragged the cart through. I was supposed to go to the storage rooms and get more Gatorade, but I couldn't stop thinking about what Trey had said. Why would Coach retire?

He wasn't old enough. And his team was having a banner year. Why walk away from that?

Maybe he doesn't want to retire, I thought. *Maybe*

Dr. Roque got his way, after all. Maybe the college board is getting rid of him. Maybe he's just quitting before they can fire him.

Had we been too quick to dismiss Dr. Roque as a suspect?

It was only a rumor. It wasn't a big lead. But the game was happening, and the conspiracy was actively trying to lose. We were about to seriously fail in our mission. I was willing to try anything.

The locker room was empty. Manzi must've gone out to the field after he finished cleaning. Now was my best chance to do a little snooping.

I went over to Coach's office, but I didn't know where to start. The tiny room was stuffed with trophies and photos of Coach with players past and present. It all seemed normal. I turned to the desk and began searching. Nothing in the top drawer. Nothing in any of the drawers except a few copies of the team call list. The top of the desk was always bare—Coach wasn't really a desk kind of guy. John Roque spent more time sitting there than Coach Orman did.

The computer monitor was on, showing a screen saver of a mountain lion. I shook the mouse to wake up the computer. Maybe Coach had written a letter of resignation that would give me more info.

There weren't many files. The playbook was there, and the call list, and a file full of random notes on players' strengths and weaknesses. There was a file that contained a press release template. And a file with a map of the Pinnacle campus. That was pretty much it.

"Why did the college even give this guy a computer?" I wondered. He barely used it.

Then I noticed an icon in the toolbar that looked like a padlock. I clicked on it. Sure enough, an error message came up. I needed a password.

"Football," I said, typing it.

Wrong.

Pinnacle.

Wrong.

Mountain Lions.

Wrong.

I chewed on my lip, thinking. Did Coach have a family? Kids? Pets? I'd never heard anything about his private life. Everything I'd read in the papers, even before I met him, talked about how all he cared about was getting his team to win.

Win, I typed.

Wrong.

Victory.

Wrong.

I glanced at the clock. I'd been gone from the stadium for almost fifteen minutes. The guys had to be getting thirsty. They'd be looking for me soon.

Concentrate, I told myself. My eyes roamed the walls. Photo after photo of Coach Orman. Coach with college players. Coach with NFL players. Coach with celebrities at the games. Coach with newscasters.

Coach. It was all about Coach.

Orman, I typed.

There was a little trumpet sound, and then the locked folder opened. I had to laugh. Who used their own name as a password?

Inside the folder was a spreadsheet. I opened it.

Lists of names and numbers met my eye.

I knew those names. I'd seen those numbers before. It was the spreadsheet from John Roque's PDA, the one with the information about Roque's clients and how much money they'd put on the game.

I scrolled to the bottom. There were a few new names.

But what was it doing here? Why did Coach have this file? *Maybe that's what the announcement is going to be about,* I thought. *Maybe Coach is going to out John Roque as a bookie. It's a good way to discredit his dad. Then Coach could keep his job, because the col-lege board will be on his side.*

I had to hand it to the guy. It wasn't a bad plan.

"I wish you hadn't seen that," said a voice from the doorway. "Now there's gonna be trouble."

16.

Score!

"You suck, Flynn!" somebody yelled from the stands.

"*Booooooo!*" The stadium echoed with the sound. "*Booooooo!*"

We were down 24–3 in the second quarter. The fans had stopped even trying to be supportive.

Out on the field, Flynner dropped back to throw the ball. Then he waited. And waited.

"Aloia's open!" Luis bellowed from next to me. "Williams is open!"

But Flynner didn't pass. He just stood there, his arm cocked, waiting for the defensive linemen to fight their way through to him.

"Sack!" somebody in the stands groaned as Flynner went down.

I shook my head. The dude wasn't even trying to make it look good. He should have thrown over one of the receivers' heads, or at least pretended to trip so that there would be a reason for him to get sacked.

"Take him out!" yelled another fan.

"Get rid of Flynn!"

"This is the worst we've done all year," Luis muttered. "We've been down before, but never by more than two scores."

"The defense is really stepping up, though," I pointed out. "If we can keep Miller State from scoring, we can still come back in the second half."

"Not with Flynner playing this way," said Luis. "The fans are right. Coach should take him out."

"Coach should've taken him out a quarter ago," the guy on the other side complained. "Flynner's been playing this whole game like he's never held a ball before."

A roar went up from the crowd as Flynner handed off to Marco. People were on their feet, cheering, hopeful. But I knew it was all a waste. If one of the other running backs had the ball, there was a chance that something good could happen. But Marco would just find a way to mess up.

Sure enough, he ran right into a wall of Miller State guys. The run was over.

"Ah, man, there was a hole the size of Jupiter to the right," one of the tackles moaned. "Even I could have found my way through there! Why did he go straight?"

"What is this, Pop Warner?" somebody heckled us from the stands.

"Do something, Coach!" another fan yelled.

I looked at Coach Orman. He was staring intently at the field, frowning.

"Why doesn't he put you in instead of Flynner?" I asked Luis.

"I don't know." My suitemate sounded frustrated. "I know I'm not the big star Flynner is, but I can play a lot better than him today."

Coach motioned to the refs for a time-out. "Flynner, Aloia, Muñoz," he called. "Get your butts over here."

Finally! I thought. *He's going to do something about this.*

"Offense, gather round," Coach barked. The offensive line surrounded Flynner and his coconspirators.

"Hardy, that's you," Ken told me from his seat on the bench. His ankle was wrapped and elevated on a cooler. "You're the kicker now."

"Oh. Right." I hurried over and squeezed in between two big guys.

"I don't know what is going on out there," Coach was saying. "All I know is this: The entire country is watching this game right now, and they're all thinking that the Mountain Lions are a mess. Flynner, Marco, Anthony." He jabbed his finger at each of them in turn. "You guys don't even look as if you're trying."

None of them met his eye.

"I thought you were smarter than that," Coach went on. "At least make an effort."

Flynner nodded. So did Marco. But Anthony just stared at his cleats, miserable.

"Now get back out there," Coach growled.

The guys all pulled their helmets on and jogged onto the field. I couldn't believe it. Coach left Flynner in the game. Sure, he'd yelled at the guy a little. But it wasn't enough. It wouldn't save the team from losing.

I sat back down next to Luis.

"Only a few minutes left before the half," he said miserably. "I bet they score again."

He hadn't even finished the sentence when Flynner lobbed the ball to Anthony, even though Anthony was surrounded by Miller State linebackers. One of them shoved Anthony to the ground while another jumped into the air, caught the ball, and ran.

"Come on," Luis groaned. "Why would you throw to a guy who's so heavily covered?"

We watched, resigned, as the Miller State dude practically skipped down the field and into the end zone. Our field position had been so bad to begin with that he didn't have far to go.

Boos rang out across the stadium when the touchdown points went up on the board.

Flynner pulled off his helmet and wandered over to the bench. "Where's the Gatorade?" he complained. "I'm thirsty."

Everyone stared at him, shocked. It was as if he didn't even notice that we were getting trampled. *He notices*, I thought, bummed. *He just doesn't care*.

"Get rid of him, Coach!" a voice echoed through the air.

"No more Flynn!" somebody chanted.

Several other fans picked up the chant. "No more Flynn! No more Flynn!"

Coach Orman frowned. He went over to Flynner and spoke into his ear. Was he finally gonna throw the idiot out?

"Check it out!" yelled Ken, pointing to the field.

I swiveled my head around just in time to see two of our huge defensive tackles take down the Miller State kicker. The ball was in the air, and a third humongous Mountain Lion leaped at least five feet straight up. He reached as high as he could, got his fingers on the ball, and smacked it to the ground.

A huge cheer went up.

I heard myself yelling along, a big grin on my face.

"Big whoop, we blocked the extra point," somebody murmured behind me. I glanced over my shoulder—at Anthony. He wore a sour expression on his face.

"This crowd will take what they can get," I said quietly. "You guys are making sure they don't have much to cheer about."

He frowned at me. "I tried to catch that pass. I *tried*. There were four guys on me." He pulled on his helmet and stalked back onto the field.

I flashed back to the most recent interception. Had Anthony actually gone for the ball? I couldn't remember. Maybe he was having a change of heart. Maybe watching the team lose was worse than the idea of his blackmailer calling the Ethics Board.

Miller State's kick was pretty good. We only managed to get to their forty on the return. The next play was another handoff to Marco. Flynner executed it perfectly. But Marco ran for about a yard, then stumbled and fell on the ball.

"Lame," Luis commented.

The second-down play was a pass. Flynner threw a beautiful spiral to Farley, one of the receivers. He was tackled immediately. Still, it was a gain of eight yards. And Flynner seemed to be back on his game. Whatever the coach had said to him must've gotten through somehow.

I knew it wouldn't last, though. As they set up for the third down, I saw Flynner grab Anthony's face mask to pull him in close. They had a little private conversation on the field, and I had a feeling I knew what it was about. Flynner was saying it was Anthony's turn to mess up.

Just as I expected, it was a pass. Flynner threw to Anthony. Anthony caught it cleanly . . . and then he ran. Ball tucked against his side, arm out front to block, he ran full-out. Our guys sprinted to help him, taking down Miller State players left and right.

I couldn't believe it. Anthony was going for it, for real! Then a Miller State dude jumped over a tackle and hurled himself through the air at Anthony. They fell in a heap at the twenty yard line.

People in the stands cheered loudly. It had been a great run.

As the offense set up for the first down, I saw

Flynner shove Anthony. Anthony ignored him. Then Marco shoved him too. Anyone else who saw them probably thought they were congratulating him on the good play, but I knew better. They were yelling at him for doing a good job.

On the first down, Marco ran into a pile of Miller State defenders. No yards gained.

On the second down, Flynner threw the ball away even though he was nowhere near being sacked.

Right before the third down, Coach suddenly called a time-out. "Hardy!" he yelled over to me. "Get out there!"

"What?" I asked.

"Field goal attempt," Coach said. "Now's your chance to show us you belong here. Luis, you go hold the ball for him."

"But it's only third down," I replied. "Shouldn't we try for a first down? Shouldn't we go for the end zone?"

"Usually, yes," said Coach. "But the way we're playing today, we won't get it. And you'll most likely miss on your first try. So I'm giving you two downs to score."

"That's crazy," Ken put in. "You can't attempt a field goal twice."

"It's unorthodox," Coach agreed. "But we've

got nothing to lose. Get out there, Hardy."

I had no choice. I grabbed my helmet and jogged out to the field. The goalposts loomed up in front of me as I set myself up behind the line of Mountain Lions.

Just like in practice, I told myself. *I got it through a couple of times there, and this is no different.*

But it was totally different. In practice, the guys coming to flatten me were my teammates. Here, they were a bunch of really gigantic, mean-looking strangers. In practice, the stands were empty, and nobody really cared if I missed. Here, the stadium was filled with eighty thousand people, all of them super-invested in me kicking through those posts.

The sound of the crowd was unreal. From out on the field, I could hear it from all sides, a low throbbing roar.

Tune it out, I ordered myself. *Concentrate on the ball and the posts, nothing else. It's a short field goal. You can do it.*

Luis yelled, "Hike!" And suddenly everything was moving—the ball flying through the air to Luis. Our offensive line running forward. Miller State's huge guards sprinting toward me.

Then the ball was on the ground, Luis holding it steady.

I didn't have time to think. I ran, my eyes on

the ball. At the last second, I looked up at the goal-posts. I aimed . . . and kicked.

The ball flew through the air. A big guy grabbed me around the waist and hurled me to the ground, knocking the wind from my lungs.

But I kept my eye on the ball—as it went straight through the goalposts.

"Field goal!" somebody yelled.

Field goal! a voice inside of me echoed. I'd done it! I'd scored! I had actually kicked a field goal for one of the most famous teams in college football!

I ruled.

My teammates yanked me off the ground and began hugging me and smacking me in the head and shoving me around joyfully. I laughed out loud, I was so happy.

"First field goal?" somebody asked.

"Yeah," I replied, grinning.

A hand grabbed my face mask and jerked me forward. Flynner's face was right in mine, snarling. "It better be your *last*, too."

 FRANK

I raised my eyes from Coach's computer screen— to see John Roque standing in the doorway.

"Roque," I said. "Aren't you supposed to be out on the field?"

"Coach told me to see what was taking you so long," said Roque. "And now I see."

"I was just checking—," I started.

"Save it," Roque snapped. "I can see the monitor from here, loser. I know what you're looking at."

I'd never heard his voice sound so nasty before. And I couldn't help noticing that the guy was blocking the door. The entire door.

How come I never realized how big he is? I wondered. Roque might be a techie, but he had his father's football-player build.

Under the desk, I hit the Record button on my ATAC surveillance device. I didn't know where this was going, but it couldn't hurt to have a record of it.

"Okay, okay," I said, holding up my hands. "You caught me. I know this is your spreadsheet. I know you're a bookie."

"Yeah? So?" Roque growled.

"Look, I found this spreadsheet on Coach's computer. In a locked personal folder. I think he's planning to go to the press with it," I told him.

"What?" Roque's eyebrows shot up. "Why would he do that?"

"Your dad is trying to get him fired. If he discredits you, he'll also discredit your father," I explained. "Then the college board will have to side with him, not your dad."

"Wow," said Roque. "You're not too bright, are you?"

I didn't know what to say. I am pretty bright, in fact.

"Coach Orman is the bookie, loser," Roque told me. "I just keep track of things for him. And I make sure he doesn't get caught."

I stared at him, the pieces falling into place. "The electronic voice when people call, that's you hiding Coach's identity."

"Obviously." Roque leaned against the door frame. "I've only been working with him for a couple of years, but I've already taken his operation to the next level. I think I'm going to do fine when he's gone."

"Huh?" I asked.

"Didn't you hear? Coach is retiring. Why else would he bring out the big guns like this?"

"The big guns." My head was spinning. "You mean the conspiracy? Throwing the game?"

Roque shrugged.

"You *are* the one who's been blackmailing Anthony Aloia," I said. "We thought you were. But then your dad didn't know about it."

"My dad's not too bright either," Roque replied.

"You're doing it for Coach, not for your father," I realized. "Coach is the mastermind we've been looking for.

"You knew all along," I said, realizing the truth. "You knew Joe and I were undercover."

"Nah, I didn't know until I caught you hanging around in the locker room that night," Roque

SUSPECT PROFILE

Name: Thomas "Tip" Orman

Hometown: Sarasota, Florida

Physical description: 46 years old, 6'1", 212 lbs.; broad shoulders, graying hair.

Occupation: Head coach for the Pinnacle Mountain Lions

Background: Played college football for Pinnacle; has coached college ball ever since.

Suspicious behavior: Takes bets on college football.

Suspected of: Masterminding the conspiracy to throw the game.

Possible motive: Greed.

admitted. "You and your idiot brother were obviously lying. So I asked Coach about it and he told me who you were."

"Wow. He didn't tell you right away? Guess he must not trust you very much," I mocked him.

"Coach likes to keep things to himself. He believes in giving out information on a need-to-know basis." Roque shrugged. "It's one of the things I learned from him. The less you know, the less you can tell other people."

"That's why Anthony and Marco don't even know who Flynner's so-called friend is," I guessed.

Roque rolled his eyes. "*Flynner* doesn't even know who his 'friend' is. He got the electronic voice calls like everyone else. He just wanted to act like a big shot." Roque twisted his head to the side, cracking his thick neck. "Coach will tell Flynner if he needs to. Otherwise, Flynner will just take the money and never have a clue who gave it to him."

I shook my head, disgusted with all of them. "I can't believe that Coach Orman is the mastermind of this whole thing. He's the last person we would have suspected."

"That was the idea. Too bad you didn't find him in time," Roque sneered. "The game is lost already, it's just a technicality now."

"We were trying to keep Pinnacle from losing,"

I said. "But Coach Orman's scheme is a crime, whether they lose or not. I can expose him after the game and he'll be in just as much trouble. Actually, he'll probably be in more trouble."

Roque frowned.

"I mean, if the team loses on purpose, Coach will be guilty of defrauding everyone in the stands and everyone who placed money with him. If the team wins, he's only guilty of conspiring to defraud them. It's just a technicality. . . ."

"Why do you want to be that way?" Roque asked, suddenly nice. "We don't have to fight. We can do business. There's a lot of money coming our way after this game."

"How much?" I asked.

"More than a hundred thousand," answered Roque.

Wow, I thought.

"Each."

Double wow.

"So we can cut you in," Roque said. "Obviously we can afford it."

"But I don't get it," I told him. "Coach had a winning season. Why not just keep doing what he was doing? Why is he retiring now? Why this whole conspiracy?"

"You met my dad," replied Roque. "He hates

Coach Orman. He wants to get him fired, and he finally got some of his cronies to admit that Coach was their bookie. He gave their statements to the college board."

"So Coach thought they'd fire him?"

"They'll totally fire him," Roque said. "They just didn't want to do it until after their precious football team won the championship."

"That's pretty low," I admitted. "So Coach wants to lose just to get back at them?"

"I guess it's a nice side effect," Roque responded. "But it's really about the money. He's got to retire anyway, or they'll fire him. And if he tries to get a job somewhere else, they'll rat him out about the gambling thing. His career is over no matter what."

"He figured he might as well make some money on the way out," I finished for him.

"It's only fair."

"No, it isn't," I shot back.

"They're gonna ruin the guy's reputation!" Roque argued.

"He's been gambling on a sport that he's involved in," I pointed out. "He's a bookie! It's a conflict of interest. And it's also illegal."

"Whatever." Roque stood up straight and crossed his huge arms over his chest. "Are you in or not?"

"First tell me something," I said. "Why are *you* doing this? Coach is your father's enemy. Why are you working for him?"

"Do you know what my father cares about?" Roque asked. "Football. Oh, and football. And also? Football. You know what he doesn't care about? Me. Not since eighth grade, when I decided I didn't want to play anymore. I hate football."

"So you're involved in an illegal gambling ring and a conspiracy to commit fraud just because your father ignores you?" I asked. "You're the one who's not too bright."

Roque stepped toward me, his broad shoulders blocking my view of the door. "Is that a no?" he demanded.

"Oh, yeah," I said. "That's a no." And then I charged him.

17.

A Good Tackle

Flynner held on to my face mask, his eyes two inches from mine. "I don't like this game you're playing, Hardy," he snarled. "You're supposed to be helping me, not kicking field goals."

"You know what, Flynner?" I replied. "I'm not your number one fan anymore."

I threw my weight to the side, pulling him off balance. He let go of my face mask just in time for me to jerk my neck back and head-butt him.

Flynner stumbled backward.

"Fight!" somebody yelled.

"Knock it off," I heard Coach bellow.

But I wasn't stopping. I'd had enough of this big bully. Maybe we hadn't found the mastermind behind the conspiracy, but we definitely knew Flynner was in on it.

That was enough for me.

I yanked off my helmet. People were reaching toward us, getting ready to pull us apart. I only had a split second.

Flynner took a swing at me. I stepped into his blow, ducked under his arm, and grabbed him around the waist. My forward momentum took us both down, Flynner falling backward.

Into the equipment cart.

It crashed onto its side with the two of us on top of it.

"I never played kicker before," I said. "I'm really a tackle."

"Get off me!" Flynner cried, trying to shove me away.

His movement set the cart off balance. It slid out from underneath him, one corner of the metal frame popping up into the air. I jumped to my feet, but Flynner wasn't so fast. The bent metal corner left a long, deep scratch in his arm as it moved.

"Ow!" Flynner yelped. He jerked his arm away, but it was caught between the side of the cart and the bottom. Instead of getting away from it, he pulled the entire thing over onto himself.

We all heard a disgusting *crunch*, and then Flynner was howling in pain.

The team doctor came running, while I grabbed the cart and pulled it off the quarterback. Coach Orman knelt by his side.

"That's broken," Ken said from behind me. He stood on his one good foot, leaning his weight on Luis's shoulder. "I can see it from here. The arm's bent all weird."

He was right. Flynner's forearm was at the wrong angle. No wonder the guy was yelling so much.

"I didn't mean for him to break something," I said.

"You didn't do that. He did it to himself," replied Ken. "And he deserves it. He pushed me into that cart on purpose."

"There's no way he can play," the doctor told Coach. "He needs to get to a hospital and have that bone set."

Coach grabbed the equipment cart and hurled it angrily away.

"I don't know what he's so mad about," Luis muttered. "Flynner's been playing all day as if he had a broken arm."

The ambulance pulled into the stadium, and the paramedics quickly got Flynner up and into the back. There was some scattered applause from the stands, but not the roar of support you'd expect for the star quarterback.

Coach just stood there, watching as the ambulance pulled away.

The refs blew their whistles to start play again. Our defense ran out onto the field. But Coach still just stood there.

"Coach?" said Luis.

Coach didn't answer.

"Interception!" someone in the stands cried.

I whirled around to see one of our safeties hit the ground, the ball cradled in his arms. My heart gave a leap. Finally, one of the turnovers was going our way!

"Coach?" Marco asked. "What do we do?"

Coach Orman looked at him. "Well, the game's probably as good as lost. Just do what you can." He turned away and went to sit on the bench.

My teammates glanced at one another. Coach was acting really weird.

"Get in there, Luis," Ken told him. "You have to."

Luis pulled on his helmet and turned to the offensive line. "What are you waiting for?" he bellowed. "We've got great field position and it's first down. Let's go score!"

He ran onto the field, the other guys behind him.

"All right!" one of the fans shouted.

"Go, Pinnacle!" somebody else added.

On the first play, Luis handed off to Marco. Marco just stood there holding the ball until one of the Miller State tackles took him down.

Great, I thought. *Luis can have all the spirit in the world, and it's not gonna help as long as Marco and Anthony are still refusing to play.*

But Luis didn't let it get him down. I saw him yell at Marco. Then he huddled up with the guys and laid out a plan.

On the second down, he dropped back and threw the ball. It spiraled into the air, heading all the way into the end zone.

Heading right for Anthony.

I groaned. Two bad plays in a row would be enough to get anybody down, especially a backup quarterback facing a tough opponent in a championship game in front of an angry crowd.

I waited for Anthony to miss the ball.

He leaped into the air. Stretched his arm up high—and grabbed the ball!

Anthony fell to the ground, clutching the football to his chest.

Touchdown!

I jumped up and down along with all the other guys on the sidelines. Anthony did it! He caught the ball clean and didn't drop it. I felt my face break into a huge smile. The dude had decided to do the right thing, after all.

Luis was already setting everyone up for the extra point. I grabbed my helmet and ran out there.

"Hardy," Luis told me when I got into the huddle. "We're gonna fake. I want the two-point conversion. This team needs a big play and we need more points on the scoreboard. I want to go into halftime with good momentum. We'll fake and I'll throw to Anthony. What do you say, man? Can you do a repeat of that last catch?"

Anthony met my eye. "Definitely."

We lined up. The play started, and I dropped back as if to get ready to kick. But when the snap came, Luis didn't set it up for me. He just grabbed the ball and ran to the right. I saw Anthony booking up the sideline, making a beeline for the end zone.

The Miller State defense scrambled to adjust.

Too late.

Luis hurled the ball.

Anthony turned at the last second, snatched the ball out of the air, and kept going straight into the end zone.

The stadium went nuts.

Two extra points—and a kick-butt play!

The Mountain Lions were back!

I rushed right at Roque.

He held up his arm, elbow locked, and thrust it into my chest.

I bounced off the big guy like he was made of rubber. The force of the blow sent me flying backward into the desk, and I struggled to get my breath.

Roque gave me a nasty smile. "If you're not gonna join me and Coach, I can't let you leave here. You're planning to tell the authorities about our little scheme. And I just can't have that."

"What are you gonna do, kill me?" I asked. "You're just some rich kid with a lot of computers. You're not a murderer."

"If it's a choice between murder or jail, I just might pick murder," said Roque.

"You're bluffing."

He shrugged. "I can make it look like an accident. I'm smarter than the cops. I know what they'll look for."

"You have a pretty high opinion of yourself," I said casually, trying to distract him.

"I—," he started.

I pushed myself off the desk and kicked both feet right at his stomach.

"Oof!" Roque doubled over.

I ran for the door.

He spun toward me and chopped me in the neck, hard.

I fell sideways and Roque moved quickly to block the door again. He was breathing hard and clutching his stomach. But he was standing.

"Just because I don't like football doesn't mean I'm a wimp," he snarled. "I've been studying martial arts for years."

"I can see that," I muttered. I hadn't expected the dude to be so tough.

"Maybe I won't kill you," he said. "Maybe I'll just injure you. You know, badly enough that you won't be able to talk afterward. You don't mind spending the rest of your life in a coma, do you?"

He spun quickly and hit me with a roundhouse kick.

I saw it coming and blocked it, but I didn't have enough room to maneuver properly. His kick clipped me in the side, and my rib cage exploded in pain.

This guy is too big, I thought. *He's stronger than me*.

"You should have taken the money," Roque said. He hit me with two quick jabs in the stomach. I blocked one, but the other one got me.

"You hurt me, my brother will just tell everyone what happened," I pointed out. "You can't kill us both."

Roque laughed. "I'm not gonna kill you, remember? I'm just gonna give you brain damage."

He sent a chop at my head, but I ducked it and hit him in the side.

"Maybe I'll kill your brother, though," Roque said, wincing from the pain. "I don't think the little kicker boy is gonna give me much trouble."

"You'd be surprised," I told him. "Joe is a pain in the butt."

Roque took a step back and dropped into a fighting stance. I automatically moved into the same stance.

What am I doing? I thought suddenly. *I don't want a karate match. I'm sick of this guy!*

I lowered my head and sprinted straight at him, yelling the whole way.

Surprised, Roque stepped forward, reaching for me. I tucked my chin against my chest and jumped at him, ducking under his arms and catching him around the knees.

Caught off balance, the dude crashed to the floor.

Before he could recover, I sat up and put my knee on his neck, holding him in place.

"I know martial arts too," I told him. "But I also know some football tackles. Maybe you should've paid more attention to your father's sport."

I reached for the phone on the desk and yanked it out of the wall. The cord made a nice rope to tie Roque's hands together. I didn't take my knee off his throat until his wrists were bound.

"I'll still pay you," he said when I moved off of him. "I'll pay you not to tell. I have plenty of money. You can have it all."

"Sorry, dude," I answered. "You threatened my brother. No amount of money makes up for that."

18.

Halftime Show

"Luis!" a reporter yelled as we walked off the field at halftime. "Over here!"

"Luis," called someone else. "How does it feel to be out of Flynn's shadow?"

"Hey, Luis! Can I get five minutes?"

"Dude. You're the most popular guy on the team," I said to my suitemate. "I don't think we're gonna make it back to the locker room. These people all want a piece of you."

Luis grinned. "They'll just have to wait. I have to get my man here to a bench before he falls on his face."

Ken rolled his eyes as he hopped along between us. He had one arm slung over each

173

of our shoulders. "It's just a sprained ankle," he said. "I could still take you."

"Doubt it," Luis retorted.

We all laughed.

"Luis, give me a statement," a woman called, sticking a microphone right in front of me and Ken.

"Please watch out for my boys," Luis said politely.

She pulled the mike back. "You're saving the team. What do you have to say?" she asked.

"We're still losing, and we've got a long way to go to come back in the second half," Luis said. "That's all I care about. I'm not gonna waste my time talking to reporters."

He kept going, ignoring all the people calling for his attention.

"Why don't you go enjoy the spotlight?" I asked.

"Yeah, Manzi can drive me back to the locker room in the cart," Ken put in.

"Dude, I'm not gonna let you ride on the cart like an invalid," said Luis. "Besides, reporters are annoying. I'm not Flynner. I'm not in it for the fame."

"At least you're in it," I told him. "Flynner's gone for good. It's all you now."

"And you," Luis replied. "We've still got another two quarters to go. Think you can pull out some more great kicks?"

I winced. "I dunno. You guys are all way out of my league. I wish Ken wasn't hurt."

"I can't believe Flynner pushed me," Ken said. "What was up with that?"

"He didn't want you to play," I told him. "That's why your lucky sweatband was gone."

"That sweatband is not lucky," said Luis. "You were wearing that smelly thing when you got hurt. I'm burning it when we get back to the dorm."

Ken frowned at me. "Hey, where did you find my sweatband, anyway? How come you had it?"

"Uh . . . I stole it from you," I admitted. "Sorry."

"What?" Ken cried.

"Why?" Luis asked, appalled.

"It's kind of a long story," I told them as we limped into the locker room. "You see, I'm not really a kicker. In fact, I'm not even in college. And neither is Frank. We're sort of like law enforcement agents. . . ."

"I can see that," Luis said, stopping in his tracks. Ken's eyes had gone wide.

I glanced up. In front of us stood about seven cops. Two of them were wrangling John Roque into handcuffs. Two were talking to Frank. One was on the radio, giving coordinates on Flynner's ambulance.

And two were waiting in the doorway, studying everyone who walked in.

"Hurry it up, boys, please," one of them ordered. "We want the door closed."

"What's going on?" Luis asked. I helped Ken sit on one of the benches.

"We don't want to tip off the coach that we're in here," the officer replied. "Everyone please stay quiet."

I glanced around the room. About half the team was back already, and they all looked baffled.

Then the door swung open and Coach Orman appeared, followed by a couple of the defensive linemen.

Coach took one look at the cops, then turned to run.

The huge guys behind him tried to get out of the way, but the hallway wasn't wide enough. By the time Coach got past them, the cops already had a hold on his arm. He struggled, but it was no good.

They dragged him back inside and into his office.

Frank came over, grinning.

"So what's up?" I asked him.

"I found the mastermind," he said. "Coach. He was the one planning to lose the game."

All the guys nearby gasped.

"What? That's crazy!" cried Ken. "Coach is the whole reason we're such a good team to begin with."

"Well, he did leave Flynner in all day," Luis said slowly. "Even though the guy was dropping balls left and right."

"Yeah . . . ," Ken agreed. "And Flynner injured me so I couldn't play."

"Flynner was in on it," I told them.

"After Flynner was taken away, Coach just kind of checked out," one of the tackles said. "Luis, you were calling the plays for the whole end of the second quarter."

"That's true." Luis frowned. "But why would Coach do that? How could he do that to his own team?"

They all looked so confused and upset. It was no way to spend halftime.

"Hey!" I yelled, jumping up on the bench. "Who cares what Coach did? You all know the playbook by heart. Who cares what Flynner did? He's out, and now we have Luis. Luis is on fire!"

A ragged cheer went up from the team.

"We still have a game to win," I added. "Can we do it?"

"Yeah!" Luis yelled.

"Can we?" I said again.

"Yeah!" the whole team roared.

"Then let's get back out there and show Miller State whose house this is!" I cried. "M-O-U-N-T-A-I-N!"

"L-I-O-N-S!" my teammates bellowed.

"Mountain! Lions!"

"Roooooooaaaaarrrrr!"

19.

A Winning Season

"One score, baby!" Luis cackled the next day. "One beautiful touchdown. That's all it took!"

"Well, one beautiful touchdown after two back-breaking quarters of clawing our way to a tie score and forcing Miller State into overtime," Joe corrected.

I bit into my grilled cheese sandwich and looked around the dining hall. Pretty much the entire football team was here. But it was the first time we and our suitemates had eaten here. Ken had decided that all his superstitions were over now that Pinnacle had won the championship. "Where is our winning receiver?" I asked.

"Anthony? He said he had a meeting this morning," Ken replied. "Why?"

I exchanged a glance with Joe. We hadn't told the police about Anthony's part in the conspiracy yesterday. But it was sure to come out. Roque and Coach might try to keep the cops from finding out that they were blackmailing somebody. But Flynner would definitely spill it. He was too dumb to realize that extortion made the charges against them even more serious.

"Uh-oh. I recognize that look. It's a secret agent look," Luis said. "What's going on?"

"We're not *secret* agents," I told him. "We're just *undercover* agents."

"And don't talk so loud," Joe added. "You two are the only ones who know the truth about us."

"What, that you have to go back to high school tomorrow?" Ken teased.

"Yeah," I said, fake-sighing. "It's not fair. You guys get to go on and have an amazing season next year as the starting quarterback and the starting kicker. And we just have to go back to our lives as agents on incredibly cool, high-octane secret missions."

Luis threw a french fry at me.

"Check it out," Ken said, nodding toward the door of the dining hall. Anthony Aloia had just walked in. And with him was Dr. Fred Roque.

"Anthony!" one of the linebackers yelled.

Everyone cheered and whistled for the receiver. Anthony motioned for them to stop, but they all just yelled louder.

Finally he smiled.

"It's about time," Joe said to me. "That guy needs to loosen up."

Anthony spotted us and headed straight over. Dr. Roque trailed behind him.

"Hey, guys, mind if we sit?" Anthony asked.

Joe's eyebrows shot up. "Both of you?"

"Yeah. That okay?" asked Dr. Roque.

"Sure." I pushed my chair to the side to make room. "But I'm surprised to see you here, Dr. Roque. I thought you'd be down at the court-house."

"My son's hearing isn't until later this after-noon," Dr. Roque said. "So I came by to help out Anthony here."

"How?" asked Joe.

"Dr. Roque came with me to see the Ethics Board this morning," Anthony explained. "I went in to tell them that I was part of the conspiracy to throw the game."

"What?" cried Luis. "But you scored more points than anyone else yesterday!"

"I changed my mind halfway through," Anthony said. "But for the first two quarters, I was mostly messing up on purpose. I had to admit that. I'm through with keeping secrets."

He's a good guy, I thought. "What happened?" I asked him.

"I told them what I did, and I told them why," he responded. "That I was being blackmailed. I guess by Coach."

"We don't think so," said Joe.

"I hate to say this, Dr. Roque, but I think it was John who did the blackmailing. At least, he did a lot of it," I told him. "He had the voice modulator. And, well, he knew that you had given Anthony's parents a bribe."

Ken and Luis sat silently, eyes wide.

"It wasn't a bribe," Dr. Roque insisted. "Those things were gifts to Anthony's parents. The car, the TV . . ."

"Inappropriate gifts," Anthony said. "My family should never have accepted them."

"And I should never have offered them," agreed Dr. Roque. "That's what I told the Ethics Board. I screwed up, and Anthony's parents screwed up. And poor Anthony got blackmailed because of it. He's a good kid and a great receiver and the team needs him. That's what I said."

"And what did the Ethics Board say?" Joe asked.

"That I can play next year." Anthony couldn't

keep the excitement out of his voice. "I'm on probation, but I can play!"

"Excellent!" Luis slapped him a high five.

"It was seriously cool of you to do that, Dr. Roque," I said to the ex-player.

He shrugged. "I really do care about the team. I guess that was always John's problem with me. Maybe I care a little too much. But I don't want the Mountain Lions to suffer because of what I did. I never meant any harm."

"My parents gave back all the stuff," Anthony added.

"Yeah, and I'm forbidden to be a booster anymore," Dr. Roque went on. "It's just as well, since my son has been asked to leave Pinnacle. Obviously I need to spend more time with him, and less time cheering for the football team." He stood up and clapped Anthony on the back. "I'm still on your side, though, guys. Good luck next season."

He made his way out of the dining hall, but Anthony stayed with us.

"Is Marco in jail?" he asked me.

"His parents posted bail," I said. "He'll be charged with fraud and conspiracy, same as Flynner. But it's less serious than what they'll hit Roque and Coach with. They've got racketeering charges, extortion, all kinds of things."

"Still, Flynner and Marco will never play football again," Ken commented.

"I can't believe it," said Anthony. "All for money."

"People do strange things," I agreed. "But the important thing is that the Mountain Lions won."

"And Frank and I accomplished our mission," Joe said. "Again!"

CLUE IN TO THE CLASSIC MYSTERIES OF THE HARDY BOYS®
FROM GROSSET & DUNLAP

$6.99 ($9.99 CAN) each

AVAILABLE AT YOUR LOCAL BOOKSTORE OR LIBRARY

Grosset & Dunlap • A division of Penguin Young Readers Group
A member of Penguin Group (USA), Inc. • A Pearson Company
www.penguin.com/youngreaders

ALL THE

SPY GEAR™

BOOKS WILL SOON BE REVEALED

Spy them now

BOOK 1:
The Secret of Stoneship Woods

BOOK 2:
The Massively Multiplayer Mystery

BOOK 3:
The Quantum Quandary

BOOK 4:
The Doomsday Dust

Be on the lookout for

BOOK 5:
The Shrieking Shadow